The Clue on the Silver Screen

The sound of music filled the theater, and the credits started to roll on the screen: *"A Day in the Country,* a film by Joseph Block."* As the credits faded, a long panning shot of a city came on the screen.

Suddenly Nancy heard a terrible, deafening explosion. Then the screen went blank.

Nancy ran to the door of the projection booth. Opening it, she saw a narrow smoke-filled staircase leading up into darkness. She leapt up the stairs and entered a small, dark room. The projectionist lay on the floor, his eyes shut. She bent down to feel his pulse. He was breathing.

Then Steven Forelli burst into the booth. He turned to look at the projector. He let out a deep groan. "It can't be!" He flung open the cupboards beneath the projector.

"What are you looking for?" Nancy asked.

"The film," he muttered tensely. "There were four reels of *A Day in the Country*—and they're all gone!"

Nancy Drew
Mystery Stories

Available from MINSTREL Books

123

NANCY DREW®

THE CLUE ON THE SILVER SCREEN

CAROLYN KEENE

A MINSTREL® BOOK

PUBLISHED BY POCKET BOOKS

New York London Toronto Sydney Tokyo Singapore

A MINSTREL PAPERBACK *ORIGINAL*

A Minstrel Book published by
POCKET BOOKS, a division of Simon & Schuster Inc.
1230 Avenue of the Americas, New York, NY 10020

Copyright © 1995 by Simon & Schuster Inc.
Produced by Mega-Books, Inc.

ISBN: 0-671-87206-0

First Minstrel Books printing February 1995

10 9 8 7 6 5 4 3 2

NANCY DREW, NANCY DREW MYSTERY STORIES, A MINSTREL BOOK and colophon are registered trademarks of Simon & Schuster Inc.

Cover art by Aleta Jenks

Printed in the U.S.A.

Contents

THE CLUE ON THE
SILVER SCREEN

1

Troubled Waters

"Bess, wake up! We're here!" George Fayne said, looking out the window as the bus pulled into the dockside parking lot. She shook her sleepy cousin by the shoulder.

"The sea air is famous for putting people to sleep," said Nancy Drew, who was sitting across the aisle. "But George is right—this is no time to doze. Come on, Bess, wake up!" The three girls had traveled from their home in River Heights, and had finally reached their destination: the small Cape Cod harbor of Woods Hole.

As Bess roused herself, the girls gathered their belongings and emerged into the late-morning bustle of the busy Cape Cod dock. Half a dozen cars were already lined up, waiting to move onto the ferry. Several foot passengers stood on the dock, waiting with their suitcases.

Staggering off the bus, Bess sleepily brushed the blond hair from her eyes and yawned. "Buses always make me sleepy."

George rubbed her hands together briskly. "It's chilly out here. I could really use something hot to drink. Why don't I try to find us some tea?"

"Yes, tea or hot chocolate would be great. Thanks," Nancy said. While George headed for the snack bar beside the ticket office, Nancy and Bess gazed out at the choppy waters of the harbor. A huge ferry was just backing into the dock, several gulls swooping and squawking above. Big doors opened in the ship's hull, and a line of cars began to drive out. Meanwhile, people were walking down from the upper decks on a metal gangway.

Once the ferry was cleared, the boarding quickly began for the forty-five-minute trip back to Martha's Vineyard, a large island south of Cape Cod. "Where on earth is George?" Bess asked worriedly, looking around for her cousin. "If she doesn't hurry, we'll miss the ferry."

"Here I am," said George, appearing at her side. With her was a young man who was carefully holding a cardboard tray with four containers of hot chocolate. He was tall and lanky, with untidy sandy-colored hair and a friendly manner. He smiled a lopsided grin at Nancy and Bess, gesturing for them to help themselves.

"This is Bill Zeldin," George said. "He's going to the Martha's Vineyard Film Festival, just like we are. He knows all about the films, and he works for that film critic—you know, the famous one—"

"Slow down, George! Let's get in line first," Nancy interrupted, laughing. As they joined the passenger line, Nancy smiled warmly at Bill. "Hi, I'm Nancy Drew, and this is Bess Marvin."

Bill smiled and shook hands with Nancy and Bess. "Are you in the movie business?" he asked.

Nancy smiled and shook her head. "Not at all," she replied. "My dad got complimentary passes for us. He's a lawyer, and one of his clients owns a chain of movie theaters. We're just ordinary people who like movies."

"How refreshing!" Bill declared. "In my job I meet too many movie people. All their gossip and backbiting gets to me after a while."

After handing their tickets to the ticket collector and tossing away their hot chocolate cups, the girls and Bill climbed the metal ramp onto the ferry. Bess looked around excitedly at their fellow passengers. "I'll bet there are lots of famous people on this boat," she gushed.

Bill craned his long neck to scan the crowd on the passenger deck. "Looks like old Robert Hastings is here," he said. "I would've thought he'd fly to the Vineyard. It's more his style."

"Who's Robert Hastings?" Nancy asked, following Bill's line of vision.

Bill pointed to a heavyset, dark-haired man in a pin-striped suit. "He runs the Ohio Festival of Film

3

in Yellow Springs every summer," he explained. "He's a pain in the neck to deal with. My boss—I work for the film critic Joan Staunton—has been battling with him for years. He doesn't like critics; he thinks they have too much power." Bill winced. "And after our last encounter, I'm not so sure he'll be happy to see me."

"Why? What happened?" Nancy asked curiously.

"Well, he had called Joan for some information about a famous director," Bill said. "People are always calling Joan with questions like that—she's written quite a few film biographies and reference books. She asked me to do the research at the film library we use in New York. It took longer than I'd expected, and when I called Hastings back with the answers, he was furious! He said he'd needed the information *immediately* to make an important decision. You could say he's difficult."

George looked puzzled. "If he runs his own film festival in Ohio, what's he doing here?"

Bill shrugged. "He probably thinks it's a good idea to check out the competition," he said. "Besides, rumor says he tried to snatch Velma Ford away from the Vineyard Festival, and he lost out."

"Who is she?" George asked. "Never heard of her."

"Yes, you have," Nancy said. "She was a star in those old-time silent movies."

"George, you didn't read the film festival schedule that Nancy's dad gave us," Bess chided her cousin. "Velma Ford starred in several movies by Joseph Block, the director they're honoring this year. She's speaking tonight at the opening of the festival."

"Why don't they get Block himself to speak?" George asked.

"Because he's dead, silly," Bess responded. "Those movies were made ages ago. And apparently, he had a tragic early death." Bess sighed dramatically.

"I happen to know a lot about Block. Joan is writing a biography of him, and I've helped her with the research," Bill put in. "He died in a car crash in 1929. And right after that, Velma Ford retired, even though she was only twenty-three years old. She'd worked with other directors, but Block was the one who'd made her a star. I guess after he died, she lost interest in acting."

Just then Bill's eyes brightened. "Speaking of Velma Ford—I'll bet that's her!" He pointed across the deck at a fragile-looking elderly woman. She wore an ankle-length velvet coat and a huge black satin hat, with a dark veil hanging over her face.

Bess gasped excitedly and grabbed George's arm. "It's her!" she said in a stage whisper.

"Shhh!" George said, disentangling herself from her cousin's grasp. "She'll hear you!"

The woman slowly but grandly made her way toward one of the deck chairs in the bow of the ferry. A cluster of people trailed behind her. As she lifted her dark veil, the girls glimpsed a white face with large, heavily made-up eyes and scarlet lipstick outlining a bow-shaped mouth.

"She looks incredible, doesn't she?" Bill murmured. "I've only seen rare pictures of her for the past sixty years. She stays inside her New York apartment. She hasn't left it for years."

Bess sighed and said, "It's so romantic. She sounds like Greta Garbo. 'I want to be alone!'" Bess put her hand to her forehead in a melodramatic gesture.

"She just went off to be by herself?" George asked. "She must have been lonely."

Bill nodded. "She probably was, from time to time. But she chose that exile for herself. The Hollywood studios asked her to come back repeatedly, and Broadway producers tried to get her to appear on stage. But she always said no."

"Did she have a companion?" Nancy asked.

"She's had a series of paid companions over the years," Bill answered. "Well-trained, of course—they don't talk to the press. That young woman in the glasses, walking behind her and carrying a blanket, is probably her current companion."

They watched as the elderly star seated herself on the deck chair. Her young companion settled the actress comfortably and laid a plaid mohair blanket over her legs. A group of people hovered around, one offering coffee, another asking for an autograph. It was like a small court of admirers paying homage to a queen.

As people came and went around her, it was just possible to catch fleeting glimpses of Velma Ford. Nancy thought she had never seen such an odd and magnificent outfit. Beneath the velvet coat was a flowing silk dress, colored with deep blues and purples. Her tiny feet were encased in black satin high-heeled slippers.

"I'll bet everyone on this ferry is going to the festival," Bill spoke up, interrupting Nancy's reverie. "Tourist season on Martha's Vineyard doesn't start until June, and I can understand why. It's freezing out here! Why don't we all sit inside, where it's warmer."

The girls agreed, and they followed him inside through a steel door into the snack bar. They ordered tea and muffins at the counter, then took their food over to a table.

As they sat chatting, the door swung open. Nancy and her friends saw Robert Hastings enter the room, deep in conversation with a woman. Hastings sounded angry.

"If Velma Ford is going to bless this festival with her first appearance in sixty years, she'd better watch her step," Hastings was saying. "I have a feeling things won't turn out the way she thinks. In fact," he added with a nasty grin, "I wouldn't be surprised if the edited Block films aren't at all what she expects."

"What does he mean by that?" Nancy asked after Hastings had moved out of earshot.

"I don't really know," Bill said, looking at the festival director with a thoughtful expression. "I did hear that Robert Hastings was bargaining with Cameo Studios to get first dibs on the Joseph Block films. Maybe he knows something we don't about the way they were finally edited."

"Edited?" George asked. "I thought those movies were made ages ago. Why would the studio edit them now?"

"All old movies have to be restored eventually," Bill explained. "The material that films used to be printed on—nitrate stock—falls apart with age. The restorers cut the deteriorated film frame by frame and remount it on modern stock, then rephotograph it. They use a computer to fill in what's missing with computer graphics."

"Wow!" George looked impressed.

Bill nodded. "It's amazing what they can do. There's even a new way to reprocess the film to eliminate the jumpy quality of the old silent movies."

"You're kidding!" Bess said. "You mean, like the way Charlie Chaplin used to walk, all jerky and speeded up? I thought that was because the movie cameras were so primitive."

"No, Charlie Chaplin's walk looked perfectly normal when the movies were first made," Bill said. "So you see, the restorers can really add a lot to an old movie. Unfortunately, while they're working on the movies, they sometimes cut and rearrange scenes, too. Anything's possible."

Just then Bess gasped, almost choking on her blueberry muffin. "Look over there! I'm sure I've seen that guy before. Isn't he a rock singer?"

Bess was staring at a handsome young man who had just walked into the room. His thick brown hair was tied back in a ponytail, and he was dressed all in black.

Bill shook his head. "You're close, but he's not a musician," he said. "He's a producer, and his name is Henry Block. In fact, he's the great-grandson of Joseph Block, the director we were talking about earlier. Maybe he'll speak at the opening event, too." Bill grinned and added, "But I bet he's also here to look for potential investors. Young producers are always hard up for money."

Soon the ferry began to slow down, and Nancy, George, and Bess rose to collect their suitcases. Bill stood up and said, "It's been nice meeting you, girls. Have a great time at the festival."

Nancy said, "Thanks for filling in the background for us. Maybe we'll see you at the opening event this evening." Bill shook their hands and left to pick up the backpack he'd left on the lower level.

The girls came out onto the outer deck. Leaning on the rail, they watched the ferry backing into its slip at the Vineyard Haven dock. Then they headed down the gangway into the town of Vineyard Haven. Edgartown, where the festival was based, was in another corner of the triangle-shaped island.

Shading her eyes, Nancy looked around for the car-rental office where they would pick up their car for the week. She quickly spotted it right across the street, in the middle of a row of shops. Bess and George waited on the dock with their luggage while Nancy trotted over to get the car.

As she swung the red rental car up the street leading to the dock, she saw Bill Zeldin chatting with the cousins again. She pulled up, and Bill leaned down to speak to her. "Do you think I could hitch a ride with you?" he asked. "I'm planning to rent a bike in Edgartown, but I have to get there first." He grinned and readjusted his heavy backpack.

"Sure, no problem," Nancy said. She fumbled for the trunk-release button and popped open the trunk lid. Bill and the girls loaded their bags in the trunk, then they all climbed in and set off.

Nancy drove and George navigated, studying the map in the travel guide she had brought. The road to Edgartown was like a leafy tunnel, with tall oak trees arching overhead.

As they pulled into Edgartown, Bess admired the graceful nineteenth-century houses lining the main street. "I had no idea Edgartown would be so beautiful," she said, pointing at an ornate white building fronted by Grecian columns.

"It's not what I expected," Nancy agreed.

"When I heard the festival was in a seaside resort, I didn't picture anything as New Englandy as this."

"Could you drop me at the corner of South Water Street?" Bill asked. "That's where my hotel is." He scrabbled in his jacket pocket and took out a folded piece of paper. "Here it is: the Harbor House Hotel."

George located South Water Street on the map, and they dropped Bill off at a large, imposing hotel overlooking the harbor. They made plans to meet in the lobby of the theater where the first film was to be shown that evening.

George spotted their hotel, a 150-year-old former whaling captain's house called the Lookout Inn, on Main Street. Early spring flowers brightened the flower beds in front of the white clapboard house. Cheerful flowered curtains hung in the bay windows on either side of the front door. As they entered, Bess cooed over the beautiful antiques in the lobby.

As the girls were about to check in, there was a sudden commotion behind them. "Did you really think you could get away with this, Mr. Forelli?"

Nancy turned to see Velma Ford, her eyes blazing, confronting a short, balding man with a mustache.

Nancy whispered, "That must be the festival director. I wonder what has Ms. Ford so upset?"

Steven Forelli was doing his best to calm down the irate actress. "I assure you, Ms. Ford, we didn't

11

know until the last minute that the studio had sent this re-edited version."

"I demand that you withdraw this film and replace it with another!" Ford declared in a throaty, dramatic voice. "If you don't, I'll make sure that your opening night will be an evening you'll never forget!"

2

Opening Night Disaster

"Ms. Ford, please believe me, I had nothing to do with this!" Steven Forelli protested. "Do you think I would have kept something this important from you?"

"I don't know and I don't care," Velma Ford declared haughtily. "All I want from you now is your word. Will you withdraw this film from the festival?" As she spoke, Velma Ford's emerald green eyes sparkled angrily.

"But, Ms. Ford, be reasonable," Forelli began. "You can't possibly expect me to withdraw the single most important film of the festival."

The star threw her head back and laughed bitterly. "Of course I can. Now please get out of my way!" Pushing her way past the festival director, she stormed out of the hotel.

Steven Forelli stood stunned for a moment at the front desk. Then he trotted off after her.

"What do you think?" George asked. "Does this mean tonight's movie won't be shown?"

Nancy drew the festival calendar out of her shoulder bag. "*A Day in the Country*—Block's masterpiece," she said, reading the description. "What could this new version have that's upsetting Velma Ford so much?"

"I guess we'll find out tonight," Bess said.

"We've barely arrived, and already there's a mystery," George teased. "Leave it to Nancy Drew to find a mystery wherever she goes."

Nancy smiled modestly. An amateur detective, she had involved the cousins in plenty of exciting investigations. But she had hoped that this trip to a charming island would be just for fun. "Let's check into our rooms," she suggested. "I doubt there's any mystery here."

After dropping their bags in their rooms, the three girls enjoyed a late lunch in the hotel's dining room. Afterward they strolled out onto Main Street to browse through the shops and boutiques in its white clapboard buildings. Above the sound of cars and the general street noise, sea gulls could be heard, their cries a constant reminder of the harbor just two blocks away.

The shops had something for everyone. One store displayed handmade colonial doll houses, with miniature furniture correct down to the smallest detail. A toy store specialized in beautiful train sets running on tracks that wound snakelike around the shop. George was delighted by a camera store that had dozens of antique cameras on display.

As dinner time approached, the girls returned to their inn to change. "Why don't we have dinner at the Harbor House restaurant?" Bess suggested as they entered their lobby. "Bill said lots of big names at the festival are staying there."

"Star-gazing, Bess?" Nancy teased her friend.

"Well, it *is* supposed to have a great view of the water from the dining room," chimed in George, looking at the entry for the restaurant in her guidebook. "And it's just around the corner."

"Okay, then," Nancy agreed. "Just so long as we get to the theater by seven-thirty. We don't want to miss the opening night." Recalling Velma Ford's threat to Steven Forelli, Nancy felt an irresistible tingle of curiosity.

The film festival theater was a few blocks from the Harbor House, in a beautifully preserved building designed in the 1920s. As the girls arrived, a large crowd was already gathering in front. Most people were dressed for the occasion, men in dinner jackets and women in evening clothes.

Bess tugged nervously at the skirt of her light blue floral-print dress. "I hope this is dressy enough," she whispered, eyeing the red satin floor-length gown of a raven-haired woman.

"Don't worry, Bess," Nancy said soothingly. "You look great. In fact, I think we all look fine."

15

She was wearing an elegant dark green silk dress that set off her blue eyes, and George was wearing a navy blue linen pants suit. She added, "A lot of these people are show biz types. They're supposed to look like that. Half of them are probably here looking for jobs."

George grinned. "I think you're right, Nan. Look over there." A bearded young man, decked out in a sequined top hat and tails, was posing for a picture.

The girls made their way through the crowd and into the lobby. The festival offices were on the ground floor, while the theater itself was on the second floor, up a long curving staircase. As they climbed the stairs, Nancy glanced at the film posters lining the walls.

"Look at that," she said, pointing, to George and Bess. "One of the original posters for the film we're about to see—*A Day in the Country*." The poster showed three young women in 1920s clothes, looking out the window of an old steam-powered railroad car. The girl in the middle was very beautiful, with short gleaming dark hair, large eyes, and a bow-shaped mouth.

"Hey, they look like us!" Bess exclaimed. "There's George, in the middle with the dark hair, and Nancy with the blond hair, and me, the chubby one on the right!" Bess giggled.

"The one with dark hair is Velma Ford, isn't it?" George asked excitedly.

They flowed with the crowd into the jam-packed theater lobby upstairs. An ornate golden chandelier hanging from the ceiling cast a soft glow over the people below. The floor's thick carpet muffled their footsteps.

The girls found it impossible not to overhear bits and pieces of the conversations around them: gossip about movies, actors, directors, or producers. Everyone there seemed in the know.

"Look, there's Bill," Bess said, nudging Nancy and gesturing toward the far corner of the room. "Let's go say hello."

The three pushed through the throng to where Bill stood, eyeing the bustle with a smile.

"Hello again," Bill said as Nancy, Bess, and George arrived. "Isn't this fantastic! It's one of my favorite sights in the world—people gathered together to see a great film."

"I read the summary of the movie in the program," Nancy said. "Three city girls spend a day in the country, having adventures and getting into trouble. Is it supposed to be a comedy?"

Bill cracked his knuckles in obvious enjoyment of his knowledge. "Not really, at least not slapstick, like Charlie Chaplin or Laurel and Hardy. Its humor is sophisticated. *A Day in the Country* was made in 1927—filmed on Martha's Vineyard, actually. Block had a summer house here, and he loved the island. Like all of his movies, it was a silent film."

"When did they start using sound in films?" asked Bess.

"The first 'talkie' was in 1927—a movie called

17

The Jazz Singer," Bill explained. "It was a huge hit, and all of a sudden all the studios wanted nothing but talking pictures. Block was one of the last holdouts."

"That's weird. You'd think he'd have welcomed sound. It's so much more realistic," said George.

"Well, maybe," Bill said. "But Block felt silent films were more artistic because they depended completely on the actors' faces and gestures to show emotion. The actors almost had to be mimes, to get across their feelings."

Bess frowned. "In the silent movies I've seen on TV there's *some* dialogue," she noted. "The picture cuts to a black screen with words printed on it, to tell you what they're saying."

"Yes, but the best silent movies, like Block's, didn't need many of those dialogue cards," Bill said. "The actors' faces, the dramatic lighting, the set design—that's what told the story."

"So I can see why an actress like Velma Ford would prefer to work with someone like Block," George murmured.

Bill nodded. "But in the end the studios got their way. They added soundtracks to all of Block's films, even though he was against it. He never forgave them for it."

Bess looked outraged. "How could they just make up a soundtrack?" she asked.

"They used actors to dub in the voices, and they put in sound effects: doors slamming, wind blowing, rain falling, horses neighing, and so on," Bill said.

18

"And they added a complete musical score. It changed the entire feeling of the film. When I was in film school, I saw the original, silent version of this movie. The one they're showing tonight has the soundtrack. I'll be interested to see the difference."

Nancy bit her lip, recalling the argument between Velma Ford and Steven Forelli. That must have been why the actress was so mad—she shared Block's hatred of movies with soundtracks.

"Some of Block's earlier films are scheduled for later in the week," Bill went on, "and I know that at least a couple of them are in their original form. So you have a treat in store."

Just then the double doors leading to the theater were swung open by a team of ushers. The crowd began to file in eagerly, and the auditorium was soon packed. Nancy and the others took the only seats together they could find, at the back of the theater in front of the projection booth.

The theater was large and beautiful, decorated in authentic 1920s art deco style. The girls sank down onto soft plush crimson seats.

As Nancy took the aisle seat, she noticed Henry Block, Joseph Block's ponytailed great-grandson, sitting in the row behind her. He seemed restless, shifting in his seat uncomfortably.

"By the way," Bill mentioned, "my boss, Joan, will be introducing the film."

"But what about Velma Ford?" Bess asked in surprise, trading glances with Nancy and George.

Bill shrugged. "She backed out at the last minute.

19

I'm not sure why. Joan and I had to spend all afternoon throwing together a speech. It's good publicity for Joan, though, with her new biography of Block being published soon."

Before Nancy could tell Bill about that afternoon's scene with Ford and Forelli, the gold velvet curtains on the stage parted. Steven Forelli stepped out to welcome the audience. After a few opening remarks about the festival, he spoke about Joseph Block's genius. Then he introduced Henry Block, Joseph Block's great-grandson. Block stood up, looking ill at ease, and bowed slightly to the audience. He quickly resumed his seat.

Next Forelli introduced Joan Staunton, a tall graceful woman dressed in a black silk pants suit, a sort of modified tuxedo. She wore her dark hair pulled back in a sleek ponytail, and striking make-up accented her large, dark eyes.

"I know some of you expected Velma Ford to be here tonight," Staunton began. "But unfortunately, Ms. Ford was unable to be with us." A low murmur of disappointment rose from the audience.

Joan continued, "But her absence should not spoil your pleasure in this film. This version of *A Day in the Country* is unique. An extra ten minutes of film has been added to the end, ten minutes that have never been seen before."

This time the murmur that rose from the crowd was one of excitement. Nancy glanced over at Bill, who flashed her a smug grin, delighted at the effect this information had on the audience.

"The footage was found recently in Cameo Studios' storage vaults, apparently left there after Block's death by his cameraman," Joan went on. "The studio's restorers decided to release it as part of this film. They weren't too sure where to fit it in, since it uses completely different locations from the rest of the movie. But that doesn't matter. The discovery of this new work by a great master is an exciting event in itself, like finding bootleg tapes recorded years ago by a rock band like the Beatles."

Joan finished her remarks, and the lights went down. Nancy settled into her seat with a contented sigh. She loved movies, and this one was bound to be a thrilling experience. The sound of music filled the theater, and the credits started to roll on the screen: "*A Day in the Country*, a film by Joseph Block." As the credits faded, a long panning shot of a city came on the screen.

Suddenly Nancy heard a terrible, deafening explosion. Then the screen went blank.

For a few seconds the audience sat in shocked silence. Then everyone started babbling at the same time. Nancy was already on her feet, running back to the door of the projection booth.

Opening it, she saw a narrow smoke-filled staircase leading up into darkness. She leapt up the stairs and entered a small, dark room, with one small window overlooking the theater below. In front of this window stood the projector, its spools still spinning with a loud clatter.

The projectionist lay on the floor, his eyes shut.

21

Gray smoke and soot covered his face. After swiftly checking around for flames, Nancy bent down to feel his pulse. His chest rose and fell with his breathing, she noted with relief.

Then Steven Forelli burst into the booth. He helped Nancy raise the projectionist's head. The man opened his eyes and sat up shakily.

Forelli turned to look at the projector. He let out a deep groan. "It can't be!" He flung open the cupboards beneath the projector.

"What is it?" asked Nancy.

Forelli didn't answer for a moment as he frantically tossed aside old playbills and empty film cans, covering the same space over and over.

"What are you looking for?" Nancy repeated.

"The film," Steven Forelli muttered tensely. "There were four reels of *A Day in the Country*—and they're all gone!"

3

Vanishing Act

"Someone has stolen the movie!" Steven Forelli moaned, obviously distraught.

Nancy's attention was drawn by a harsh scraping sound above her head. Looking around the dimly lit projection booth, she spotted another narrow steel staircase leading upward, probably to the roof of the building. She charged up the stairs, her heart pounding.

In the shadows above her, she heard a door slam against metal. At the top of the stairs, she found a rusty trapdoor in the ceiling, still standing open.

Lifting herself through the door, Nancy came out onto the roof of the building. The moon was not yet up, and it was almost completely black outside. As her eyes adjusted to the dark, she could hear the thud of footsteps running away across the wide, flat roof. She took off in that direction.

Suddenly, silhouetted against the night sky, a dark figure balanced on the parapet at the edge of the roof. Nancy could just make out a slim shape in dark pants and a jacket. Had she imagined it, or could she also see a dark ponytail?

The figure was there one instant, gone the next. Nancy thought for one terrible moment that the person had jumped off the roof. But as she raced to the edge of the building and looked down, she could see metal glinting in the light from the nearest streetlight. The metal was a fire escape, leading down the side of the building. The dark figure was jumping from the bottom rung and running down the alley alongside the building.

Nancy was halfway down the fire escape when a harsh, clattering sound came from below. Looking down, she could see that the person had knocked over several garbage cans, blocking the alley.

Nancy halted. She could never catch up now, she realized with frustration. Wearily she climbed back up the ladder. I'll try to talk to the projectionist, she decided. Maybe he'd seen something, maybe even the thief's face.

By the time she returned to the projection booth, the police had arrived and were talking to Steven Forelli. The festival director whirled around when Nancy came down the steps. "Did you find the thief?" he asked anxiously. "I must have those film reels back!"

"I'm sorry. It was too dark to see anything," Nancy admitted.

A female police officer, Raye Garvey, asked Nancy who she was. Nancy explained, describing what she'd seen on the roof and offering her help in the investigation.

The policeman who seemed to be in charge of the investigation, Officer Poole, nodded thoughtfully as Nancy explained that she was a detective. "Lucky for us we have a trained pair of eyes on the scene," he said.

"Do you know what caused the explosion?" Nancy asked Poole.

"Well, we're not sure yet, but it looks like a simple cherry-bomb device," Poole said. "Very amateurish, but it did the job." He held up a small, sharp piece of wood. "The projectionist says that when the explosion happened, something hit him on the head. We think it was a piece of wood like this, probably from the cupboard door over there." He pointed to the storage cupboard. "We think that's where the bomb was planted. Anyway, it knocked him out for a few moments, long enough for the thief to steal the film and get away."

Nancy nodded. "Do you need to talk to me any more?" she asked.

"You can go," Poole said. "But will you let us know if you can remember anything else?"

"Of course," Nancy said. "And you can reach me at the Lookout Inn if you have any questions."

She returned to the theater to find Bess and George waiting for her. Steven Forelli followed her. "Ms. Drew," he called. She stopped and turned to face him. "Can I have a word with you after I make my announcement?" he asked.

"I'd be happy to," Nancy agreed. Nodding, Forelli then threaded through the chattering, excited crowd to the front of the room.

The girls took their seats, and Nancy quietly told Bess and George what had happened.

An expectant hush fell as Forelli mounted the stage and began to speak. "I must apologize for this unforeseen interruption," the shaken festival director began. "There's no need for alarm. We had a slight mishap in the projection booth, and as a result, we will not be screening *A Day in the Country* this evening."

There were loud murmurs of surprise, together with anger and disappointment.

"I know many of you came especially to see this famous film, and we will do our best to schedule another screening later in the festival," Forelli went on. "But for now, I ask you to be patient. We will resume the festival tomorrow at noon with the published schedule of events. Thanks, and good night."

Forelli gestured for the audience to leave by the back exit doors, and people reluctantly began to collect their belongings. There was a loud discontented buzz in the theater as Nancy, Bess, and George watched the audience file out.

Steven Forelli came up the aisle to where the girls were sitting. "Excuse me, Ms. Drew," he said, looking uneasily at Bess and George.

Nancy quickly said, "These are my, uh, assistants, George Fayne and Bess Marvin." Bess and George nodded eagerly. The director gave them a half-smile and sat down in the row in front of them, turning to face them.

"You're our only eyewitness," he told Nancy. "I know you couldn't see the thief's face, but maybe you'll remember something later. Anyway, I thought it might help if you knew something about the background of this situation."

"Of course, I'd appreciate anything you could tell me," Nancy said.

"The studio has another copy of this film," Forelli explained, "but this one was specially edited for its showing at the festival. I'm afraid it will cost the festival a huge amount of money to replace it."

Forelli looked up grimly at the theater's blank, silvery screen. He continued, "Anyway, as I've explained to the police, it all started about six months ago, when the first mailings for the festival were sent out. I started receiving these letters from Robert Hastings." Forelli paused.

"He's the director of the Ohio Festival of Film, isn't he?" asked Nancy.

"Do you know him?" Forelli asked.

"No," Nancy said. "But he was pointed out to me on the ferry trip over."

"Oh, I see," Forelli said. "Well, in the past, the Ohio Festival has never been competitive with the Martha's Vineyard Festival—our agenda has always

27

been different. Up until this year, we focused on showcasing new films, particularly by young directors. The Ohio Festival has always been a revival showcase: that is, they revive old films and hold seminars on film history."

Forelli pulled a wrinkled linen handkerchief out of his pocket and mopped his damp forehead before continuing. "As you can imagine, when we announced we were going to showcase Joseph Block's films this year, Hastings decided we were trespassing on his turf. Of course it's not like that! There are festivals all over the world that duplicate each other's efforts." Forelli was getting worked up as he spoke. His face started to turn red.

Nancy tried to calm him down. "He does sound unreasonable," she murmured.

"First he threatened me with a lawsuit," Forelli said, "and when that didn't work, he said he'd do whatever he could to make sure my festival was a failure." Forelli wiped his forehead again, then stuffed the damp handkerchief in his pocket.

Just then Nancy noticed Joan Staunton approaching softly from the back of the theater. The film critic lowered herself elegantly into the seat beside Forelli. Patting him soothingly on the arm, she said, "What a shambles! What a hard time you're having, darling."

Forelli looked at her, startled, and said, "Joan, this is Nancy Drew and—"

"And George Fayne and Bess Marvin," Nancy

28

finished. "We were just talking about what happened here tonight."

"Nancy was a witness," Forelli added. "And, luckily for us, she's a detective."

"Oh, I see," Joan replied, smiling at Nancy. "I believe Bill Zeldin mentioned you girls to me. Didn't you meet on the ferry?" As Nancy nodded, she continued. "I heard Steve telling you about Hastings and his bad attitude toward the festival. I can support that with a few little stories of my own. The man's a menace!"

Forelli nodded grimly. "He really got mad when I managed to get Velma Ford to come out of retirement to speak here," he added. "Apparently he'd been trying for years to get her to speak at his festival, with no luck."

"But in the end, she didn't speak here either," George pointed out.

"Oh, that's another problem altogether," said Forelli. "The two aren't connected."

Or were they connected? Nancy wondered to herself. Velma had been upset about tonight's film. One way or another, what she wanted had happened: the film wasn't shown. Nancy was determined to investigate further.

For now she simply said, "Maybe I should find out where Hastings was at the time of the theft."

Forelli nodded wearily, saying, "Yes, I think he's the most likely suspect. Try the Harbor House hotel. A lot of film people are staying there."

"I'm staying there. I could walk you over," Joan said helpfully to Nancy.

"Thanks," Nancy said, "but we know where it is—we had dinner there." Turning to Forelli, she added, "I'll let you know tomorrow if I find out anything." Nancy shook the man's hand, and she, George, and Bess left the theater.

As they came out into the cool evening air, George said, "Don't you think we should talk to Joan some more about Hastings? She said she could tell us some nasty stories."

"Yes, absolutely," Nancy agreed. "But I'd rather track down Hastings while the trail is still fresh. And could you and Bess check on Velma Ford's whereabouts during the screening?"

Bess looked surprised. "Nancy, you don't really think that frail old lady could have stolen the film and escaped over the roof, do you?"

Nancy shrugged. "No, but I'd still like to know where she was," she said. "We saw her earlier in our lobby. Maybe she's staying at our hotel. Meanwhile, I'll go to the Harbor House to check on Hastings. We can meet in the Harbor House lobby afterward. Okay with you?"

Bess and George agreed, and the cousins headed back to the Lookout Inn. As Nancy turned the corner toward the harbor, the old Edgartown lighthouse became visible, its beacon illuminating the nearby landscape. Nancy could see several yachts rocking gently in the harbor. A group of older people passed her, talking in shocked tones about the events at the film festival.

But as Nancy reached the Harbor House steps, she spotted a tall figure dressed in black, hurrying along the boardwalk leading to the harbor. Nancy paused, her detective instincts alerted. Something about that figure didn't look right.

Then she drew in her breath sharply. Just visible under one arm was a large round package—the exact size and shape of a movie reel!

4

A Circle of Suspects

Nancy took off after the dark-clothed figure heading toward the end of the pier. The rotating beam from the lighthouse lit the nighttime scene with an eerie quality. Shadows jumped out at Nancy as she treaded softly on the boardwalk.

Remembering the silhouetted figure on the theater roof earlier, Nancy thought how similar the two figures were, in the dark, at least. Both wore pants and a jacket, but she couldn't tell whether the slim shape was male or female. As the figure turned, though, she thought she saw a short ponytail—just as before!

Just then Nancy stepped on a loose plank. It creaked harshly through the damp air, and she froze. But luckily for her, the sound was lost in the cries of the gulls circling overhead.

The figure swung up a short ladder onto one of

the large yachts. Nancy ducked behind a wooden post. She saw a cabin door open with a crack of light. The person stepped through it, disappearing below decks.

Inching quietly along the pier, Nancy reached the yacht. She could just make out the name— *Joseph B.* Could that stand for Joseph Block? She glanced carefully around. No one in sight. She crept aboard stealthily.

Nancy knelt near the cabin door, listening intently. Two men were talking, their voices muffled by the sound of water slapping against the boat. Nancy could just barely hear them.

"I know you think it's risky," said a husky baritone voice. "But I need to do this for the sake of everyone involved. Can't you help me?"

The other voice mumbled in reply. Nancy couldn't make out what he was saying at all.

Suddenly she heard the steps inside the cabin creak. Someone was coming back on deck! She scrambled behind a mast and crouched down.

She saw one figure emerge—a man dressed in a black suit. Nancy gasped as the lighthouse beacon lit up his face. It was Henry Block!

Judging from his size, Nancy felt sure it had been him carrying the big round package. But he didn't have it now. He must have left it below.

Henry hopped off the boat and started back up the pier toward the shore. Nancy huddled in the shadows, torn. Should she wait here to look for the round package and risk being found by Henry's companion? Or should she follow Henry and see where he went next?

Nancy's instincts told her to look for the round package now and track down Henry later. She returned to the cabin door, straining her ears to hear inside. She decided to bluff her way through if the person inside tried to stop her.

Drawing a deep breath, she pushed open the cabin door. She saw a small room with a built-in sofa and a coffee table, but no one was there. A faint sound of running water and rattling pots came from behind a gleaming wood door at the far end. The galley, Nancy guessed. A narrow passageway beside the galley door led farther into the boat. With any luck, she could search the other cabins.

There was nothing in the tiny front room, Nancy quickly ascertained. She moved softly through it into the passageway.

As soon as she entered the next cabin, she saw what she was looking for. Lying atop an old oak table was a large, round plastic case.

Nancy moved swiftly to the table, unsnapped the case, and looked inside. There were four metal film cans, the kind she had seen earlier in the projection booth!

Just then she heard someone whistling in the front cabin. Whoever had been in the galley was heading this way!

Nancy snapped the case shut, then quickly flattened herself against the wall beside the door.

She heard someone step lightly down the passage-way and enter the next room down.

Her heart pounding, Nancy slipped out of the cabin and dashed back on deck. She jumped off the boat without a sound. Pausing on the shadowy pier, she could still hear the whistling below, then rock music as a radio clicked on.

She had been so close to finding out what those film cans contained! But she didn't dare go back on the yacht. I'll tell Officer Poole what I found, she decided, striding back toward shore. He could get a warrant to search the boat.

Nancy headed back to Harbor House to find George and Bess. As she entered the brightly lit lobby, she pulled up in surprise. There was Henry Block, at the front desk!

Nancy hung back, watching as the clerk handed the handsome young producer a couple of pink phone-message slips. As he read them, he jingled the change in his pocket nervously. Finally, he moved toward the elevator.

Acting casual, Nancy walked toward Henry. With a deft move, she bumped into him. "Oops!" she said loudly. Startled, Henry dropped the pink slips. Nancy stooped to pick them up, quickly glancing at the messages. One was from Robert Hastings, and the other was from Velma Ford!

He smiled awkwardly. "I'm so sorry," he said. It was the same husky voice she'd heard on the yacht, asking the other man for help. "I've got to learn to watch where I'm going."

"Don't be silly, it was my fault," she said, handing the message slips to him. "I was looking for my friends and I— Oh, you're Henry Block, aren't you? I recognize you from the screening tonight."

All the while, her mind raced. Robert Hastings and Velma Ford were both enemies of the festival. Could Henry be involved with one or both of them in stealing the film? If only she had been able to identify what was in those film cans!

Just then Bess's voice called out, "Nancy!" She turned around to see George and Bess walking toward her. "There they are," Nancy said to Henry. "I knew they were here somewhere."

"Well, it was nice bumping into you," Henry said. He headed into an open elevator.

Joining Nancy, Bess and George stared at Henry as the elevator doors shut. "Wow, Henry Block— what a hunk!" Bess sighed.

"He may be a hunk," Nancy said, "but he also may be our culprit." Nancy told them what she had heard and seen aboard the yacht, and what she had seen on the message slips.

"On the boat, I felt sure I'd caught our thief," she summed up, frowning. "But talking to him just now, I got a feeling that Henry isn't the criminal type. He wasn't nervous when I picked up those phone messages. He didn't act as if he had anything to hide."

George regarded Nancy thoughtfully. "Those hunches of yours are usually right," she noted.

"Even if they're not exactly scientific," Nancy

added with a rueful grin. "Anyway, let me go call Officer Poole and tell him what I found. If he can search the boat, we'll have a real answer, not just a hunch."

Nancy found a public telephone in the lobby, near the front door. When Poole came on the line, Nancy explained what she'd seen. He promised to check it out immediately.

Nancy returned to Bess and George, who were sprawled on a comfortable sofa nearby. "Poole's going to search the ship," she told them, "but meanwhile let's keep working. Did you find Velma Ford?"

"Yup," Bess said. "That's why we came here. The clerk at the Lookout Inn said she was here, having a late dinner. We haven't had a chance yet to talk to her, though."

"Great!" Nancy said. "First let me check on Hastings, then we'll go see Ms. Ford."

Nancy walked over to the desk clerk. "Excuse me, could you tell me if Robert Hastings is staying here?" she said.

"Yes," the clerk said, "but he's not in right now. Would you like to leave a message?"

"Do you remember what time he left the hotel this evening?" Nancy asked.

The clerk shrugged. "Sorry, I can't monitor all our guests' comings and goings."

"Thanks, anyway," Nancy said. Checking the clock on the wall, she saw that it was ten o'clock. Returning to Bess and George, she said, "The desk

37

clerk's no help in checking Hastings's alibi. Maybe some of the other staff noticed when he left tonight, but they'll be off duty now. I'll ask them tomorrow. Let's find Velma Ford."

The three girls headed for the dining room where they'd eaten a few hours earlier. Now it was dark outside, and the superb harbor view showed only a few tiny lights winking around the moored boats. Candles in glass bowls flickered on the tables, which were covered in white linen.

Velma Ford was sitting alone at a window table, staring out across the water at Chappaquiddick Island in the distance. The dining room was almost empty, so it was easy for the girls to find a table next to the actress. As they sat down, Nancy leaned over to Velma and said, "Isn't the view beautiful!"

Velma didn't respond at first. There was no food left on her table, only the check on a silver tray. The actress held an emerald green fountain pen in her gloved hand. She signed the check with a flourish. Then she turned to Nancy. "Beautiful indeed," she said in her low, throaty voice.

Nancy smiled at her. "You're Velma Ford, aren't you?"

Velma nodded again with a slight, graceful tilt of her head. Nancy waited, but Velma stared back out at the ocean. Well, thought Nancy, she really is a silent actress!

"We were sorry you didn't speak at the screening tonight," Nancy persisted. Still no reply. Finally, Nancy tried the direct approach. "Did you know

38

the film was stolen from the projection booth? We never got to see it."

Velma Ford rose slowly, with a dramatic swirl of her silken skirt. She glared darkly at Nancy. "It's a good thing that film was stolen," she declared. "If they had dared to show it, Joseph Block would have turned in his grave!" With that she wheeled and stormed out of the dining room, leaving behind her a cloud of heady perfume.

"Whew!" George exhaled. "What an act!"

"I don't know," Nancy mused. "She must have a good reason for feeling so strongly about the film. I think we should try her again tomorrow."

The next morning dawned bright and springlike. "At last," Nancy thought as she drew the curtains, "sweater weather!" Nancy always looked forward to that day in spring when she could finally shed her winter jacket.

The girls had breakfast together in the inn's airy breakfast room, set in a greenhouse overlooking the garden.

After a delicious meal of French toast, blueberry preserves, and fresh-squeezed orange juice, Bess suggested that they take the morning off to explore the island. Nancy frowned. "But I want to get on with the investigation," she said.

George shook her head. "There are no festival events scheduled this morning," she said, "so our suspects won't be around. The missing film can wait. You need some time to relax."

"Okay." Nancy gave in. "Just let me call Officer Poole first. I want to see what he learned about Henry Block." The girls adjourned to the lobby, where Nancy made her call from the front desk. After a brief conversation, she hung up with a sigh.

"The police searched Henry Block's boat," she told her friends. "They found the film cans, just where I said they'd be. But it turns out they were reels of one of Henry's own films."

"I knew someone that handsome couldn't be bad," Bess said.

"Back to square one," Nancy said, frowning.

George waved her guidebook in the air. "Sightseeing, remember? You promised, Nancy."

Nancy grinned. "All right, I surrender!"

"Let's go to Oak Bluffs," George suggested, consulting the guidebook. "There's a whole neighborhood of Victorian cottages there, painted all sorts of wild colors."

"And a carousel," Bess added, reading over George's shoulder. "One of the oldest ones in the country. I love carousels!"

"Oak Bluffs it is," Nancy said, and they headed out to get into their red rental car.

Fifteen minutes later they pulled into the parking lot near the Oak Bluffs wharf. The sun sparkled on the water, and the gulls circled and dove for fish, their cries piercing the air.

"You were right," Nancy said. "We needed some time to chill out. This is perfect."

George led the way over to Circuit Avenue, Oak

Bluffs's main street. Passing a weathered red shed, they heard tinny calliope music and saw a line of children chattering excitedly. "The Flying Horses," Bess read aloud from a sign on the shed. "That's the carousel! Let's go in."

The meaning of the name Flying Horses was soon clear to the girls as they joined the line inside. The carousel's painted and hand-carved wooden horses had real horsehair tails and manes that flowed in the air as they spun round. Rather than sitting on posts like those on most merry-go-rounds, the horses hung on rods from the top, and they swung outward as the motor picked up speed.

"What's that long bar sticking out from the wall?" Nancy said, pointing. Everyone riding the carousel leaned over to grab at the end of the bar as they whirled past.

"That's a chute full of brass rings," George read from her book. "You're supposed to grab one as you go by. If you get a gold ring, you get a free ride." She looked up, her eyes sparkling. "I can't wait to try."

"Oh, look, cotton candy!" Bess said, spotting a little girl with a sticky cone of pink spun sugar. "I haven't had that for ages. Where'd you get it?" she asked. The child pointed to a stand.

"Bess, we just had breakfast!" George protested in vain as Bess took off.

The line moved just then, and Nancy and George filed onto the merry-go-round without Bess. George chose a white horse with wild eyes. Nancy

41

picked a black horse with a white star on its forehead, just behind George.

Even though it wasn't yet tourist season, the carousel was full of excited children and smiling parents. The music started, and the carousel began to move. George shouted over her shoulder, "Don't forget the brass ring, Nancy!"

As they flew past the wall, Nancy leaned over to grab a ring and missed. She was determined to catch it next time around. The carousel was at full speed now, music braying loudly. She focused her gaze on the brass ring. "Concentrate," she muttered, poising herself on the carved saddle.

As she swung around the curve, Nancy hung on to the horse with one hand while she leaned out toward the ring. Suddenly she felt a hard shove between her shoulder blades.

Lurching forward, Nancy crashed headfirst onto the floor of the carousel. When she started to lift her head, the sharp edge of a horse's hoof clouted her on the skull!

5

Suspicious Activities

Seeing Nancy fall, the other riders on the carousel began to shout. The operator pulled a lever, bringing the carousel to a screeching halt.

Leaping off her own horse, George rushed to Nancy's side. "Are you okay, Nan?" she asked anxiously.

"Yes, I'm all right," Nancy said shakily.

Nancy was terribly dizzy, and her head ached, but at least she hadn't been knocked out. Bess arrived just as George was helping Nancy down off the merry-go-round.

"Nancy, are you all right?" Bess asked, alarmed at the bloody cut on her friend's forehead. "What happened?"

Nancy smiled weakly at Bess and touched her forehead. "It's not as bad as it could have been. Those hoofs are pretty sharp," she said. Then she frowned with concentration, trying to remember the incident. "Someone pushed me, I'm sure of it."

"But who? And why?" asked George. "I didn't see anyone around that I recognized."

"I can't believe someone would do anything so nasty," Bess declared indignantly.

"Nan, you don't think this has any connection to the stolen movie yesterday, do you?" George asked in a quiet, grave tone.

Nancy looked away, searching the milling crowd for a familiar face. "I don't know," she answered softly. "Hardly anybody even knows that I'm investigating the theft. Who would go after me, when—" She broke off suddenly.

Bill Zeldin, dressed in faded blue jeans and a bright green sweatshirt, was heading toward them through the crowd of kids and parents. What was he doing there? "Nancy, are you all right?" Bill asked, looking concerned. "I saw what happened, sort of."

"Hi, Bill. Yes, I'm okay. But tell me, what did you see?" Nancy asked.

"I only arrived just as you went down," he admitted. "But I think I saw someone leap off the carousel and run away—someone tall, in dark clothes. To tell the truth, I'm not sure if it was a man or a woman. Didn't you see who did it?"

Nancy shook her head, then winced. "Ouch, that hurts! No, I was so out of it I didn't think to ask anyone. And George was in front of me, so she wouldn't have seen the person, either."

"And I was getting cotton candy," Bess said ruefully. "I'll never eat the stuff again."

Just then a small boy with red hair and a freckled face tugged on Nancy's sleeve. "Excuse me, lady. Are you okay?" he asked.

Nancy smiled at the boy and said, "Yes, thanks. I think I'll be fine."

The boy leaned close to Nancy and whispered, "I saw who pushed you!"

The carousel operator, a pleasant-looking red-haired woman, scurried over and gently pulled on the boy's arm. "Johnny, don't bother these people," she said. Turning to Nancy, she added, "Sorry. My son gets bored sometimes, hanging around here all day."

"No, really, it's all right," Nancy said. "In fact, I'd like to talk to Johnny, if I may. He may have seen the person who pushed me." Turning to the boy, she asked, "What did you see?"

Still whispering, the boy said, "He was dressed all in black. He even had on a black cap."

Hmm, Nancy thought. The boy's evidence supported what Bill had said he'd seen, and it seemed to prove that Bill himself had not been the culprit. "Did you see his face?" Nancy asked.

"No, his cap was pulled down real low," Johnny replied. "I couldn't see his face."

"How tall was he?" Nancy asked. "Tall as me?"

"Even taller, I bet," Johnny said, his voice getting louder as he became more confident.

"As tall as me?" Bill asked.

Johnny tipped his head back to take in Bill's long, lanky frame. "Well, maybe not *that* tall," he admitted. "Not like a giant or anything."

Bill traded a grin with Nancy.

"But look at what I found," Johnny went on. He handed Nancy a bright brass button.

Nancy turned the button over in her hand. She asked, "Where did you find this?"

"Over there," the boy replied, pointing to the ground beneath the bar with the brass rings.

"May I keep this, Johnny?" The little boy nodded, and Nancy said, "Thanks for your help. I really appreciate it."

After making sure Nancy was all right, the carousel operator and her son left to switch the merry-go-round back on. Soon the cheerful music was playing again. A new crowd of children and their parents were lining up for the ride.

Nancy inspected the brass button carefully. Turning it over, she said, "It's got something engraved on it. It looks like an old-fashioned movie camera."

Bess looked at the button over Nancy's shoulder. "It's on one of those old stands they used to use—what are they called?"

"A tripod," Bill said. "Can I see?" He examined the button closely.

"He found it near where I was pushed," Nancy mused. "Maybe it fell off the clothes of the person who pushed me. I'll hold on to it for a while, just in case it *is* a clue." Looking at Bill, she added, "You look as though you recognize this button. Have you seen one like it before?"

"No," he said, "but I was thinking that it's just the kind of button a film buff might wear."

"Well, there are tons of film buffs around this week," George pointed out. "That doesn't exactly narrow the field, does it?"

"Never mind. Maybe we'll be able to track down who was wearing it," Nancy said, slipping the button into her pocket.

"And in the meantime we should get your head checked out, just in case," Bess said. Seeing Nancy start to protest, she added, "Come on, Nan, you know it could be a serious injury."

Nancy insisted that she didn't need a doctor, but she finally appeased Bess by agreeing to lie down when they got back to the hotel. Bill departed on his bike, and the girls drove back to Edgartown, with George at the wheel this time.

Bess and George offered to work on the case while Nancy rested by interviewing the Harbor House staff about Hastings's whereabouts the night before. Nancy gladly accepted their help. "But don't miss the festival film this afternoon," she added as she entered her hotel room.

"No way," Bess replied. "It's the new Hank Thompson movie, *The Emperor of Ice Cream*. He's so adorable; I've been looking forward to it."

Nancy smiled. "I meant that you should go to the festival events so you can keep an eye on our suspects," she reminded Bess teasingly. "But I guess it won't hurt if you enjoy the movie, too. I'll meet you outside the theater afterward."

After saying goodbye to her friends, Nancy went into her room and lay down. She fell asleep almost at once.

When Nancy woke up later that day, she felt much better. She sat up slowly and put her feet on the floor. So far, so good. She stood up and walked to the window. It was still light outside, which was a good sign. She looked at her watch: only five o'clock.

Nancy stood at the window, admiring the view of the hotel garden. She felt in her pocket and took out the brass button Johnny had found. What had he said about the person who'd pushed her? A man dressed in black, wearing a cap low over his face. Who could it have been? Nancy had an uneasy feeling that this had been no mere accident. But why would the thief who stole *A Day in the Country* want to hurt her?

She could rule out Bill Zeldin and Velma Ford, as neither of them matched Johnny's description. Robert Hastings was a possibility, though Nancy didn't think he knew who she was.

Then Nancy thought of Henry Block. He'd been wearing black on the ferry coming over and also at the festival the night before. When she ran into him in the Harbor House lobby that night he seemed nice, but was that just an act because he knew she was following him? When the police came later to search the yacht for the films, did Henry realize she had tipped them off?

She must check that out. In the meantime, she realized, it was time to go meet Bess and George at the theater.

Nancy dressed quickly, pulling on her jeans and a warm fisherman knit sweater. Leaving her key at the front desk, she emerged into the pale light of late afternoon. There were few people on the street as she headed for the festival building.

As she approached the theater, there was no one outside. The afternoon film obviously hadn't ended yet. She climbed the stairs to the quiet, empty theater lobby. She could hear the faint sounds of the movie being shown inside.

Suddenly she became aware of a muffled voice droning somewhere nearby. Looking around, she finally located where the voice was coming from: in the corner of the lobby was an old-fashioned wooden phone booth with a folding door. She strolled past casually and glimpsed Robert Hastings sitting inside, talking on the phone.

Robert Hastings, just the man she wanted to see. She edged closer, hoping she wouldn't attract his attention.

"Good news," he was saying. "I've got the perfect film to open our festival."

Nancy leaned closer.

Hastings continued, "Believe me, it's perfect. It's exactly what we were looking for." He paused to

49

listen to the voice at the other end. "Wait," he continued, "you won't believe this. It's better than anything you could imagine." He paused dramatically.

"I've found a rare Velma Ford picture—one that hasn't been seen in years!"

6

Over the Edge

Nancy couldn't believe what she'd heard. Could Robert Hastings be referring to the stolen film?

She edged closer to the phone booth, trying to get a good listening position. But just then the theater doors swung open, and, with a loud buzz of conversation, people poured into the lobby.

Hastings hung up the phone and pushed open the door of the booth. Darting behind a pillar, Nancy hid while Hastings walked past her toward the stairs. But just as she was about to follow him, a voice called loudly, "Nancy!" She swiveled around and saw Bess, with George standing behind her.

Unfortunately, Hastings had heard Bess, too. Turning around, he caught sight of Nancy.

It would be impossible to follow him now, thought Nancy dismally. She'd have to try to catch up with him later. Smiling weakly at Bess, she gave up the chase and walked over to her friends. "Hi. How was the movie?" she asked.

"It was really terrific!" George raved. "How does your head feel now?"

"Much better," Nancy replied. She glanced over George's shoulder at Hastings's departing figure. "Listen, guys, to what I just overheard!" She quickly filled in George and Bess.

"That proves he stole *A Day in the Country,* doesn't it?" George said. "What other Velma Ford movie could it be?"

"It's not definite," Nancy warned. "We still can't prove that Hastings has the movie. We may have to search his room or find some other hard evidence. By the way, did you learn anything at the Harbor House?"

"We lucked out," George said. "We found a maid who brought fresh towels to Hastings's room at seven o'clock. She said he had just finished shaving and was preparing to go out."

"Don't forget what she said about his mood," Bess added. "He called for fresh towels because he said his towels weren't clean. He was very rude to this maid and shouted at her to hurry."

"Thanks, guys," Nancy said. "That gives us a time frame. He left the hotel in a hurry at about seven o'clock. So he could easily have been at the theater in time to steal the film."

"Hey, could we talk about this over a meal?" Bess suggested. "The movie gave me an appetite, especially that final dinner scene."

"Ummm, yeah," George agreed.

Nancy nodded, grinning. "I must be feeling better, because I'm starving, too."

George checked in her guidebook as they headed down the stairs. "How about this restaurant at the Gay Head cliffs?" she said. "It's supposed to have a great view of the ocean at sunset."

"Sounds wonderful," Nancy said. They walked to the car, Nancy insisting that she felt well enough to drive. They took a long road leading to the western end of the island. In contrast to Edgartown, this was rural countryside, with small farms and patches of forest. Turning south to Gay Head, the road swooped up and down steep hills, revealing ponds and inlets on either side.

As they drove, George passed on information from the guidebook. "The locals call this side of the island up-island," she said. "Gay Head's an old Native American settlement. Most of the land around here is still reservation land, in fact. But what it's most famous for is the cliffs. They've even been declared a national landmark."

As Nancy drove down the last hill, the back of the cliffs loomed up ahead of them, a stout red stucco lighthouse perched to one side. The girls parked in a small lot beside the road and trudged up a steep slope, past a handful of tiny shops and snack bars, to the top of the cliffs.

"Wow!" Bess exclaimed as they reached the observation terrace. "This is spectacular!"

The Atlantic Ocean sparkled below them. The

53

sun was beginning to set, turning the sky a fierce pink, with stripes of brilliant yellow and purple. Finally, George said, "I hate to move, but I hear the view from the restaurant is just as good."

"Yeah, I can't wait to try those famous steamed clams," Bess said. They walked across the short strip of grass to the Clifftop Restaurant. After studying the daily specials written on the chalkboard, Bess and George ordered steamers and Nancy ordered New England clam chowder.

Several minutes later Bess was surveying her plate of empty clam shells. "These are the best steamers I have ever tasted!" she exclaimed.

George teased, "You always say that."

"I mean it this time!" Bess insisted.

Sighing happily, Nancy put down her soup spoon and said, "This was a great idea, George. I feel completely recovered and ready to tackle our mystery again."

George looked up eagerly. "Do you have any ideas about how to handle Hastings?"

"Not exactly," Nancy confessed. "Hastings could have stolen the film, but so many other people could have, too. And if it was Hastings, did *he* push me off the carousel? Neither Bill nor Johnny said the person was heavy, like Hastings is." Nancy stared out thoughtfully at the sunset.

"Maybe he has a partner," Bess suggested.

Nancy nodded. "Could be. Someone like Velma Ford, or even Henry Block." She paused, then added, "That brass button might help. If the person who pushed me was dressed in black, and the button came from a jacket he was wearing . . ."

"We should find out who owns a black jacket with a brass button missing," Bess said.

"Easier said than done," George said. "How can we check out every suspect's wardrobe?"

"Let's think about it," Nancy said. "There might be a way." She shook her head, as if to clear it. "Is anyone up for a walk along the beach? I could use some fresh air."

George said that she could, too. "According to the book, there's a trail leading down from the cliffs to the beach. The sunset's almost over. Let's go while there's still a view." She jumped to her feet.

But Bess was staring uneasily out at the pounding surf far below. "It would have to be a pretty steep trail to get all the way down there."

"Don't worry," George said, prodding her cousin. "I'll walk in front of you. I know you won't fall, but if you did, I'd be there to catch you."

"Well, all right then," Bess agreed reluctantly. "But the view had better be gorgeous!"

They paid their bill and made their way outside to the top of the cliffs. George found the head of the trail and led the way. After one very steep stretch at the top, it sloped off into a well-cut path, easy to follow. As it leveled out onto the beach, Bess sighed with relief.

The girls stood still in awe as the sun finally set,

with one last glorious splash of color. The sky still glowed, but dusky shadows began to gather as they walked along the beach.

Nancy suddenly pointed to the horizon. "Look over there!" she said excitedly.

In the distance, a small pinpoint of light blinked on and off, clearly visible against the darkening sky: three short flashes, followed by two long ones, then three short flashes again.

Nancy quickly took her notebook and a pen from her bag and began scribbling furiously.

"The light must be flashing from a boat," Bess said. "There's nothing else out there."

George peered over Nancy's shoulder at the pattern of dots and dashes she was writing down. "It's Morse code, isn't it, Nan?" she asked.

Nodding, Nancy kept on writing until the light stopped flashing. Then she studied what she had written. "From the point where I started writing it down, here's what I got: 'have shooting script, lie low for now.'"

Bess said uneasily, "What's a shooting script? Some kind of plan to shoot someone?"

"No," Nancy replied. "A shooting script is the director's final version of a movie script, the one he uses to shoot the film from."

"So," George remarked, "this message must be about a film someone's planning to make."

"Or a film someone has already made," Nancy added, a gleam in her eye. "I have a feeling that

that boat belongs to someone we know—like maybe Henry Block."

The girls headed down the beach, peering out to sea. They could just make out a big sailboat, moving away toward the eastern end of the island.

Eyes trained on the boat, George suddenly stumbled over a pile of charred sticks laid in a shallow pit. Wisps of smoke still rose from it, as if the campfire had just been put out. "Hey!" a nearby voice shouted.

Nancy whirled around. Standing a few yards away, near the base of the cliff, was Bill Zeldin. "Hello, Bill," Nancy said evenly. "What are you doing here?"

"I could ask you the same question," Bill said, with an odd laugh. He observed them with narrowed eyes, his usually friendly manner gone.

"Mind if we join you?" Nancy asked lightly.

Bill bent down and scooped a few final handfuls of sand onto the fire to extinguish it. "Sorry," he said stiffly, "I was just leaving."

"Would you like a ride back to Edgartown? We were about to go," Nancy offered.

"Thanks, anyway," Bill said, stuffing his hands in his pockets and staring out to sea. "But I brought my bike. It's parked up by the road."

"Well, we can at least walk back to the road together," Nancy said.

"Okay," Bill answered grudgingly. They headed silently along the dark beach, George and Bess in the lead, Bill and Nancy following.

"Listen," Bill said in a low voice to Nancy as they walked, "do you still have that button the kid found at the Flying Horses yesterday?"

Nancy looked at him curiously. "Yes, it's back at the hotel. Why?"

"I'd like to see it again," Bill said. He was about to say more, when they heard a muffled cry, as if someone nearby had tripped in the dark.

"Who's there?" Nancy asked sharply. Alerted, George and Bess doubled back to join them.

In the shadowy darkness, it was impossible to see who it was at first. Then Joan Staunton emerged from the shadows.

"Well, well, what a surprise!" Joan said, laughing. "I never expected to run into anyone else on this beach."

"We just went for an after-dinner walk," Nancy said. "What brings you here?"

"This is my after-dinner walk, too," Joan replied. "I had dinner at the Clifftop Restaurant."

"It's funny that we didn't see you," Nancy remarked. "We just finished dinner there ourselves a little while ago."

"I must have come in right after you left," Joan said, shrugging. "It didn't take me long to eat. I'm a very fast eater, aren't I, Bill? But those were the best steamers I ever had."

"Weren't they great?" Bess agreed. Joan fell into step beside Bess, launching into a lively food discussion as they headed back to the trail.

Bill fell into step silently beside Nancy. Near the foot of the trail, he pulled her aside. "Meet me tomorrow morning at ten-thirty," he muttered quickly. "In the boat shed at the Vineyard Museum in Edgartown. Alone. Bring that thing we were talking about." Then he spun around and took off, almost running, back down the beach.

"'Bye, Bill," Bess called as she watched him leave.

"I wonder what his hurry was," Joan mused, stopping. "I was going to ask him about something I need him to do tomorrow. Oh, well, maybe I can catch him. See you girls at the next screening!" She waved gaily and jogged down the beach after Bill.

"Well, that was weird," George said as the girls made their way more slowly up the cliff trail. "It was like he was avoiding us."

"Maybe," Nancy said. "He did tell me that he wants to talk to me tomorrow morning. He said to come alone. He sure is acting mysteriously."

"Do you think you should go?" George asked. "Maybe he's trying to get you on your own so he can—" She didn't finish the thought, but Nancy knew what she meant. All too often people had used violence to try to scare Nancy off a case.

"Oh, surely you don't think *Bill* is a suspect," Bess protested, puffing from climbing.

"I can't rule anyone out," Nancy told her.

The trail seemed steeper and rougher going up than it had felt coming down. "Maybe we should have gone the other way," George groaned. "The guidebook says there's another short trail going from the far end of the beach back to the road."

"*Now* you tell us, George!" Bess exclaimed.

"No, but it comes out a long way from where we're parked," George said, trying to justify herself. The two cousins went on bickering as they labored up the rest of the trail.

Nancy found herself falling behind. With the exertion, her head had started to ache again. She didn't want to complain to her friends, but she stopped a few times to breathe and steady herself.

When she finally reached level ground, Bess and George were nowhere in sight. Nancy turned around for one moment to look back at the ocean sparkling below. The moon and stars were hidden by clouds. A rising wind rustled the beach plum bushes that grew along the edge of the cliff.

But then she heard another sound, louder than the wind and somehow different. Nancy stiffened, listening intently.

Suddenly she felt a heavy blow at the back of her skull. The world seemed to tilt sideways, and a blaze of pain seared through her consciousness.

Nancy stumbled and her legs began to crumple. She was losing her footing—at the very edge of the cliff!

7

False Alarm

As if in a dream, Nancy felt herself sliding off the edge of the cliff. She swung her arms over her head, reaching frantically for something, anything to hold on to. Her fingers closed around a scraggly beach plum bush, just within her grasp.

She heard her attacker scurry away in the darkness above her head. Although the breath had been knocked out of her, she managed to call out. "George! Bess!" Her voice sounded tiny to her.

Waves were crashing below on the beach, and the wind had suddenly picked up. Nancy clung to the branch tightly, scrabbling uselessly for a foothold. She had tumbled off the trail onto a part of the cliff that sloped steeply beneath her.

Just when she thought she couldn't hold on another second, her friends appeared, George reaching down for Nancy's right arm, Bess for her left. Between them they managed to pull her up to level ground. "What on earth happened?" George gasped.

"Something hit me," Nancy said, still trying to catch her breath.

"Something, or someone?" George asked, her voice grim.

"I don't know," Nancy replied, shaken. "It felt like a large branch, or a rock." Her mind whirled. First the carousel, and now this. Who wanted her out of the way so badly?

The three girls walked back to their car, Bess and George supporting Nancy on either side. George drove as they headed back toward Edgartown.

About fifteen minutes up the road, they passed Bill Zeldin, pedaling hard up a hill on his ten-speed racer. They slowed and honked as they passed him, but he kept staring straight ahead.

"I guess he didn't realize who we were," said Bess. But Nancy frowned. She knew he'd seen them. He had deliberately not waved hello.

"Do you think that Morse message was meant for Bill?" George suddenly asked, as if she had read Nancy's thoughts. "He was on the beach."

"It could have been for Bill," Nancy said. "But Joan Staunton was also there."

"Maybe they're in this together," Bess said. "After all, he works for her."

"We have no reason to suspect Joan," Nancy pointed out. "She seemed perfectly friendly down on the beach. And what motive could she have for stealing *A Day in the Country?* Bill, on the other hand . . ." She paused. "He did ask to meet me tomorrow, to see the button again. I have a feeling he wants to give me some information."

Nancy thought to herself that Bill's behavior was definitely troubling. But somehow she couldn't think straight just then. Leaning her head back against the seat, she forced herself to relax as the car rolled through the darkness. Two accidents in one day was a bit much, even for Nancy Drew.

The next day, Sunday, Nancy awoke feeling refreshed and hungry. She met Bess and George in the breakfast room for granola, scrambled eggs, and fresh orange juice. "I'm meeting Bill Zeldin at ten-thirty," Nancy reminded Bess and George. "What are you guys going to do this morning?"

"Well," George said, "I overheard a guy at the front desk this morning who works on Henry Block's film crew. He was telling someone that Block is scouting locations for a new film. Today he's checking out a place called the Felix Neck Wildlife Sanctuary. I looked it up in the guidebook —it's supposed to be beautiful. So I thought I'd go there and see what Henry's up to."

Nancy nodded in approval. "Great. Maybe you both should go. You'll look more like innocent tourists that way," she suggested. "Talk to Henry, if you can. Try to find out if he was using the yacht last night anywhere near Gay Head. You can take the car. I won't be needing it this morning. The museum's a short walk from here."

"Nancy, please be careful," Bess said, looking with concern at her friend.

"Don't worry!" Nancy said, smiling. "I'll be *extremely* careful after yesterday."

After breakfast they made plans to meet at the next festival screening, at eleven o'clock. Then they went their separate ways.

Turning the corner from the Lookout Inn, Nancy could see ahead the cluster of white clapboard houses making up the Vineyard Museum. It was only ten-fifteen, so she wandered into the main house, browsing past displays of colonial clothing, antique dolls, and whaling equipment. Then she went out the back door and crossed a small yard to the boat shed.

Inside, the shed held a nineteenth-century fire engine and a whaleboat, a swift row boat that men from whaling ships once used to chase hunted whales. Other artifacts sat in display cases along the walls. The shed was empty, except for an attendant sitting and reading by the door.

Nancy strolled past the displays, but she barely noticed what she saw. Instead, she brooded about Bill Zeldin. She'd really liked him the first few times they met. He seemed funny, outgoing, and bright. Could he really be guilty of stealing? Or of attacking her?

64

Nancy rehearsed all the things she wanted to ask Bill. She particularly wanted to know why he was interested in the button. Maybe he had learned something about it. Nancy hoped Bill's answers would prove he'd done nothing wrong.

She checked her watch again. Ten-forty, and Bill still wasn't there. She forced herself to study a row of finely crafted Indian pots, which a sign said were once used to catch eels.

Keyed up as she was, Nancy jumped when the wail of a siren pierced the Sunday morning quiet. She listened alertly. It seemed to come from outdoors, but not too far away. Dashing to the door, she scooted outside.

People were running across the street, and Nancy could hear the siren much closer now. She ran, too, following the crowd.

As she veered onto a busier street, she realized where she was. The crowd was heading for the block that contained the festival building.

Two fire engines, their sirens screaming, roared past her and pulled up in front of the Festival Theater. Although no fire or smoke was visible, firefighters jumped out and ran into the building. Racing up to the site, Nancy spotted Steven Forelli on the sidewalk in front, clutching an armful of papers and shouting.

She ran over to the frantic director. "Are you all right?" she asked. Forelli nodded, gasping for breath as if he'd been caught in the smoke. "What happened?" Nancy asked. "How did the fire start?"

He shook his head, looking miserably at the front entrance. "I was out to breakfast, and when I came back, the alarm had gone off," he said.

Poor man, thought Nancy. It really did seem as if his festival was cursed. She was just about to question him further when the firefighters began to troop out the front door.

"False alarm," one said, taking off his helmet and unbuttoning his heavy fireproof coat. "Someone broke the glass and pulled the alarm."

Forelli looked relieved as the news sank in. "False alarm?" he repeated. "Thank goodness!"

Nancy asked the firefighter, "It's all right to go in now, isn't it?"

"Sure, no reason not to." The man shrugged. "There's no fire." Turning to Forelli, he added, "Let's hope this doesn't happen again, okay?"

"Yes, yes, of course," Forelli said, still dazed by the close call.

Nancy took Forelli's arm and walked him inside. "Maybe it would be a good idea to check your offices, just to make sure everything's okay," she suggested.

Forelli looked at her, confused. "Why?"

"Well," Nancy said, "whoever pulled the alarm might have been trying to cause more trouble for the festival. Whoever did it might have caused other kinds of damage, too."

Forelli's eyes widened. "That never occurred to me," he gasped. He looked around the ground-floor lobby apprehensively. "I'm so glad you happened to come by. Would—would you mind going through the offices and storage rooms with me? You might see something I would overlook."

Nancy, seeing that Forelli needed her, thought to herself, I can arrange another meeting with Bill later. This is more important.

It didn't take her long to find some evidence. In the main office, a large pane of glass had been knocked out of a window; the floor was littered with sharp, jagged pieces. The fire-alarm box that had been set off was directly outside the office. It was obvious that someone had climbed in and set off the alarm—someone who knew exactly where the alarm box was located.

After that, Forelli and Nancy went through all the rooms systematically, looking for theft or damage. In Forelli's office, several drawers in his filing cabinet had been pulled out, their contents scattered all over the floor.

Forelli sighed fretfully. "It'll take me hours to sort through this stuff."

"Was there anything valuable in your files?" Nancy asked the director.

"Not really. Just receipts and letters, that sort of thing," Forelli replied.

Nancy nodded. "The intruder may have simply wanted to create confusion here," she noted. "Or else he or she wanted some detailed information about the festival." Who could be interested in information like that? she considered silently. Robert Hastings, of course. But it was best not to mention that to Forelli just then.

As they entered the film library, Forelli tensed, expecting the worst. But after searching through several cabinets full of film cans, Nancy could see him begin to relax. "Our film collection seems intact, thank goodness," he said. "It took us years to collect these movies."

"What about the projection booth?" Nancy asked with a sudden flash of suspicion. "We forgot to look there."

Together they hurried up to the projection room. It took only one look for Forelli to realize what the thief had been after.

"They're gone, they're both gone!" he wailed, sinking down into the projectionist's chair. He covered his face with his hands.

"What did they get?" asked Nancy quietly.

"There were two more Block films scheduled to be shown this week: *The Bad Apple* and *Fire on the Water*. They're both gone." Forelli stared blankly at the empty storage racks.

"Can you get other copies?" Nancy asked.

"Not in time for the festival, no way," Forelli said, wringing his hands. "These were very rare prints. The studio only had one copy of each, plus the originals, in the studio's vaults in Hollywood.

But after this, you can bet they won't lend me their originals! I'll have to cancel the screenings for today," he moaned.

"I'm so sorry," Nancy said. "I'll do my best to find those films for you."

Forelli blinked and looked at her hopefully. "Is there a chance you might?" he asked.

"Well, I've got several leads," she said cautiously, "but nothing definite yet."

"I'd appreciate anything you could do." Forelli sighed. "The police don't seem to be able to get anywhere with this."

"I'll talk to them," Nancy promised. "If we share what we know, we might be able to track down the films faster." She paused, then asked, "Was Velma Ford in the two films that were stolen?"

"Why, yes," Forelli said. "But why would that be significant?"

"I don't know," Nancy replied. "I'm just checking all the angles."

Promising to keep in touch with Forelli, Nancy walked back downstairs. As she came out into the bright sunshine, she spotted Bill Zeldin by the side of the building, deep in conversation with Joan Staunton. Both of them looked upset.

Nancy hung back, waiting for Joan to leave before she approached Bill to explain about having missed their appointment. Then, out of the corner of her eye, she saw Robert Hastings. As she turned to look at him, she noticed with surprise that he had a triumphant smile on his face.

And as he turned around to speak to someone behind him, she also noticed something else. His right hand was wrapped in a white bandage, and it was stained a bright bloodred!

8

In Pursuit

Nancy stared at Robert Hastings's hand. Her mind filled with several images in swift succession.

There was Hastings as she had first seen him on the ferry, complaining bitterly about the Martha's Vineyard Festival.

Then there was Hastings sitting in the theater phone booth, gloating that he had managed to get hold of a rare Velma Ford film.

And now here was Hastings again, his hand cut and bloody—just after Nancy had found the smashed window in the festival office. She looked at Hastings's face and saw him smile that peculiar triumphant smile again.

Nancy suddenly knew that she shouldn't let Hastings out of her sight. Even though it meant not explaining to Bill Zeldin and not meeting Bess and George when they returned from the wildlife sanctuary, she had to follow Hastings.

71

Hastings left the theater building and started walking toward the harbor, whistling and with a confident stride. Every once in a while he stopped to inspect his reflection in a shop window. He smoothed his hair and straightened his tie, then smiled at himself. Nancy thought he looked as if he'd just heard some very good news.

When he turned up the steps to the Harbor House, she stayed out of sight. Once he was inside, she strolled in. He was just disappearing into the hotel's pub, an authentic old tavern.

Nancy was about to follow Hastings when she saw Velma Ford sweep into the lobby, dressed in her long velvet coat and a billowing dress of dark red chiffon. Lingering next to a potted palm, Nancy watched the elderly actress head into the pub.

Could Velma Ford be meeting Robert Hastings? Nancy wondered. She slipped over to the pub entrance and sidled in, trying to be unobtrusive.

The room was restfully dark, with low oak-beamed ceilings, a huge open fireplace, and a gleaming mahogany bar. Very few guests were there at this hour on a Sunday morning, although the harbor-view restaurant did a booming brunch business, Nancy had noticed from the lobby.

Velma glided over to Hastings's table. The festival director jumped up as he saw her coming and formally pulled out a chair for her.

Luckily, neither of them had noticed Nancy. Holding a menu in front of her face, she seated herself at a small nearby table, hidden behind a thick dark oak post. She leaned casually toward their table, trying to eavesdrop.

At first she heard nothing important. They chatted about the different kinds of coffee on the menu. A waitress came for their order, and Nancy heard Velma say, "An espresso, please. I loathe weak coffee." After the waitress had left, Velma said to Hastings, "I don't smoke anymore, thank heavens, which means I can actually *taste* the coffee, darling. It must be *perfect!*"

Just then a waitress approached Nancy, asking if she'd like something to eat or drink. Nancy ordered the first thing that came to mind: hot chocolate and an English muffin.

After the waitress had left, she settled down to eavesdropping again. She perked up when she heard Velma ask Hastings about his hand.

"My dear, that hand looks positively dreadful!" the actress said. "What did you do?"

"Oh, nothing, really," Hastings said casually. "I broke a glass this morning out at the beach house."

What beach house? Nancy wondered. Had Hastings moved out of the Harbor House into a private place of his own? She was startled to hear Velma's next words.

"I owe you a great deal, darling," the actress said. "If it weren't for you, that horrible edited version of *A Day in the Country* would have been shown. I couldn't live with that."

"Think nothing of it," Hastings said.

"But what you did was heroic!" Velma said.

"Stealing that film was the only way to prevent it from being shown. That idiot Forelli had no intention of withdrawing it, despite my pleas."

Velma paused as the waitress arrived with her espresso. "Hmmm, not bad," Velma said after her first sip. "At least Deavers could make espresso. Too bad she was so useless at everything else."

"Who is Deavers?" Hastings asked.

"That remarkably silly girl I hired to be my companion after the last one left," the actress replied. "But she got on my nerves terribly. I put her on the first ferry back to the mainland the moment we arrived. She was utterly worthless away from the city. The countryside scares her."

Nancy remembered Velma's companion from the ferry. She had forgotten the young woman until now. Evidently she was out of the picture, anyway.

"As I was saying, darling, if there's ever anything I can do for you . . ." the actress said.

"As a matter of fact, there is," Hastings said smoothly. "You can be the guest speaker at my festival on July tenth, in Yellow Springs. You know, we're doing a season of silent films this year. Of course *we* will not be showing the edited versions of great classics, only the originals." Nancy could imagine him smirking unpleasantly.

"My dear, I'd be delighted to be your guest speaker," Velma said.

Nancy couldn't believe what she was hearing. Had Robert Hastings just admitted to stealing *A Day in the Country* on the opening night? And

Velma Ford certainly seemed to approve of his theft—had she asked him to do it in the first place? Was her speaking at his festival the price she had agreed to pay for this "favor"?

Hastings was saying, "I'd love your input about the films we're planning to show. It will be so much better than what they had planned here. And with you there, it will be a triumph!"

Nancy thought of the two other Block films stolen from the festival office that morning. If Hastings had stolen the first film, she assumed he had stolen the others, too. Maybe Velma had asked him to because she didn't want those films shown, either. Or was it all Hastings's idea, just to make sure the Martha's Vineyard Festival was a total flop? If that was the case, he was certainly succeeding!

"Maybe I could speak about Joseph and the old days in Hollywood," Velma said. "After all these years, people want to know the real story, don't you think?"

What real story? Nancy wondered. But just then the waitress approached with her hot chocolate, and she missed what was being said at the other table for a moment or two.

"Don't be late, darling" were the next words Nancy heard Velma say. Peeking around her menu, Nancy saw the actress leave the restaurant. Hastings stayed behind, and Nancy decided to stay put as well. If Hastings was the man who had stolen the movies, she had to stay on his tail. She needed more than an overheard conversation before she could accuse him of the crime. Velma Ford's connection, whatever it was, could be sorted out later.

Nancy waited while the big man ordered another cup of coffee and wolfed down a piece of pie. Finally, she heard him ask the waitress for the time. When she told him, he shouted for his check and left the pub in a hurry.

Nancy followed him. She stayed out of sight but close behind as he turned toward the harbor. The street was not crowded. Tailing him would be tough, she realized.

Hastings walked briskly down the street toward the harbor. Ahead, Nancy could see the tiny three-car ferry that chugged back and forth between Edgartown and Chappaquiddick Island. Letting off a lively toot on its whistle, it was just pulling out of the dock. Hastings came to a stop and looked wildly around him. Then he wheeled around and headed for Lighthouse Beach. Nancy stuck with him.

Unfortunately, there weren't enough people on the beach at that time of year to provide her with cover. Only a few hardy sun lovers were sitting on the sand in deck chairs, trying to get an early start on their tans.

Nancy halted behind a lamppost on the board-walk, watching from a safe distance. Hastings walked toward a small lean-to a short way down the beach. It was a ramshackle wooden building and looked abandoned. Nancy was surprised when he knocked on the door. What was he up to?

The door opened a crack, and a small man with a

scraggly beard poked his head out. Quickly, Hastings slipped inside.

Nancy raced down to the beach and headed for the shack. But just before she reached it, the door opened again. Nancy jumped behind the shack just in time, as Hastings walked out again with the bearded man.

She stood as quietly as possible, trying to catch her breath and listen at the same time. But the men were silent. Whatever conversation had taken place had happened inside the shack.

The two men headed for the nearby dock, where a small motorboat was tied up. The bearded man got into the boat first and started tinkering with the motor. Hastings stood by and watched impatiently. Nancy moved out from behind the shack and walked slowly up the beach, trying not to call attention to herself.

As she came closer, she saw the bearded man motion to Hastings to loosen the tether that held the boat to the dock. Hastings did so, then got into the boat. Nancy began to walk more quickly toward the dock. What if Hastings got away?

A moment later the motor roared to life. Nancy broke into a run.

But the boat moved quickly out into the harbor. Nancy saw her quarry slipping out of her grasp.

9

Secrets in the Dark

Frustrated, Nancy looked around for another motorboat that she could use to follow Hastings. She couldn't let him get away!

At the end of Memorial Wharf she saw a couple of boats tied up and a sign advertising rentals. She raced to the end of the wharf, where a young boy was working, busily securing a boat.

"Excuse me," Nancy said. "Could I rent a boat?"

The boy pointed to a sign that Nancy hadn't noticed before. It posted the operating hours of the rental company: twelve o'clock to five o'clock. "We don't open till noon, lady," he said.

Out of the corner of her eye, Nancy could see Hastings moving farther out into the harbor.

"How much do you want for this boat?" she asked, pulling out her wallet.

The boy hesitated. Nancy could tell he was trying to figure out how much he could get.

"Here," she said, handing him two twenty-dollar bills. "Will this cover it?"

The boy nodded happily, shouting instructions about how to use the boat. Nancy jumped in, glancing over her shoulder at Hastings's boat, moving ever farther away. After a few false starts, she got the motor going and shot out into the harbor.

Nancy followed Hastings's boat as discreetly as possible, trying to catch up without attracting his attention. It wasn't too difficult, since the harbor was busy with small fishing boats and sailboats of all shapes and sizes.

Nancy could see Chappaquiddick Island, only a short distance across Edgartown Harbor. Could that be where they were heading? The ferry came churning past on its return trip from Chappaquiddick. Several people on the ferry waved happily at her, enjoying the beautiful morning. Nancy eyed the ferry's choppy wake and fought to steer her boat across it.

Up ahead, she could see Hastings and the bearded man swing their boat around to back into the Chappaquiddick dock. Nancy ducked down, afraid Hastings might see her. She waited nervously for the shout of recognition she was sure would follow.

But there was only the sound of the gulls squawking overhead. When she next looked up, she could see Hastings climbing out onto the dock.

The bearded man revved up his motor and buzzed away from the dock again, heading back toward Edgartown. He's probably a fisherman who makes extra money by ferrying people to Chappaquiddick, Nancy realized.

Nancy steered into the dock and quickly tied up her boat. Hopping out, she ran in the direction Hastings had gone, up the hill.

Chappaquiddick seemed completely different from the big island. It was much wilder, with no cute little stores selling bikinis and beach umbrellas. There were no seafood restaurants on the pier, and no expensive hotels lined the shore.

The sand dunes lining the shore soon gave way to a paved road that led uphill. The gulls circled overhead as Nancy saw Hastings disappear over the crest of the hill.

She jogged up the hill, hoping to close the distance between her and Hastings. At the top of the hill she spotted him again, up by a beach club on the left, heading toward a row of private homes. She strode rapidly after him, hoping he wouldn't turn around. On this open, sandy terrain, there was nothing to hide behind.

Hastings turned in at a single-story beach house with weathered gray wood siding. A taxi sat idling in the driveway. Hastings stopped and poked his head through the backseat window. Nancy walked quickly, hoping to get close enough to see who was in the taxi.

But she didn't have to be close to recognize that dramatic figure in the long velvet coat that Hastings helped out of the cab. It was Velma Ford.

Just then Hastings turned and seemed to look straight at Nancy! She sprinted behind a large stand of pine trees across the road.

Nancy peered through the branches, praying that Hastings hadn't seen her. She saw him take some keys from his pocket, open the door, and usher Velma Ford inside.

Once the door was shut, Nancy ran straight to the house. She worked her way around it, peering through windows into the darkened interior. She could see nothing, only an occasional glimmer of light. The side of the house that faced the water had a continuous row of tall windows—to take advantage of the view, she guessed—but venetian blinds had been pulled down tightly behind them all.

Finally, around the corner she found a large, high window that had been hidden by a scrub oak. She stood there on tiptoe, peering inside. The window was covered by a venetian blind, but a narrow gap had been left between the bottom of the blind and the window ledge.

At first she couldn't figure out what she was seeing, as the light kept shifting. Then it dawned on her that she was watching a film, projected on a huge screen. Suddenly the screen went black, and words in white letters stretched across it. It must be a silent movie, she realized.

Was this *A Day in the Country*? Or was it one of the other two stolen films by Joseph Block?

A face filled the screen, and she recognized it

immediately from the poster in the festival lobby. It was the face of the young Velma Ford, radiantly beautiful, staring into the camera.

Nancy felt stunned, seeing that young face so soon after having seen the older Velma in person. She continued to stand on her toes at the window for several minutes, her legs aching from the effort. Still, she couldn't see enough of the movie to identify it.

Dropping from the window, Nancy sat down to think. The best course, she decided, was to confront Velma there, in Hastings's house. If they were involved together in the theft of the films, she might surprise a confession out of them.

Gathering her courage, she walked to the front door and rang the bell. There was a long wait, then Hastings answered the door himself.

"Sorry to bother you, Mr. Hastings," Nancy began, improvising quickly, "but the hotel has sent me to escort Ms. Ford back to Edgartown when she is ready."

For a moment Hastings simply stood there and stared at her, his face expressing his confusion. Finally, he stepped aside and opened the door wide. "Oh, well, come in then," he said. "Ms. Ford and I are still conducting our business, but you can wait, I suppose."

Thank goodness, he hadn't recognized her! Although there was no real reason why he would, Nancy had been a bit worried. She followed him into the darkened living room.

Along one wall ran the series of windows, blinds closed, that she'd noticed outdoors. A portable movie screen had been set up at the end of the room, in front of an immense stone fireplace. A film projector at the other end shone the silent movie on the screen. Velma Ford was sitting in an armchair, staring intently at the movie. Robert Hastings moved back to the white leather sofa next to Velma's chair, where he sat down, leaning attentively toward her.

Nancy seated herself gingerly on a black-leather-and-chrome chair that proved to be as uncomfortable as it looked. Looking around the room, trying to see things in the semidarkness, she noticed a stack of film cans on a low table next to her. She was dying to get a look at their labels, but she knew she had to be careful.

Flicking a glance at Hastings to make sure he wasn't watching her, Nancy leaned sideways toward the table. Her face still turned politely toward the screen, she strained her eyes to the side and managed to read the labels on the film cans. The missing films' titles were *Fire on the Lake*, *The Bad Apple*, and *A Day in the Country*. From what she could see, those weren't the titles on these cans. Had Hastings changed the labels?

Suddenly a flash of white light covered the screen. Nancy stirred, startled. She hadn't realized the movie was ending. Hastings switched on a table lamp next to him, murmured something softly to Velma, and then rose to tend to the projector.

Velma's face looked white and drained, but she gazed over at Nancy with perfect composure. "The hotel sent you, did they?" she said to Nancy. "When shall we leave?" Then, lifting her chin, she regarded Nancy coolly with her large green eyes. "I believe I recognize you."

Nancy's heart skipped. Velma went on, "Yes, that reddish blond hair—you were in the Harbor House restaurant the other night, weren't you?"

Nancy smiled. "Yes, that's right. My friends and I asked you why you had dropped out of the festival."

Velma gestured dramatically with her right hand, indicating that there were things Nancy couldn't possibly understand. "Oh, you know, one changes one's mind sometimes. Things happen to make life impossible." She smiled a slight, secret smile and looked at the projector, whirring as the film rewound. "But one door closes, another opens. You should always remember that."

Nancy said, "I will." She was amazed that Velma didn't ask why the hotel had sent her. The actress seemed to take it all in stride, as if it had been planned. Well, that certainly made things easier.

"You look tired," Nancy said to Velma. "I came here on the ferry by foot, but I thought it would be easier to go back by cab."

"But of course," Velma replied. "I suppose I should have asked the taxi that brought me here to stay and wait, but the driver was so horrid. He was most unpleasant about having to wait so long for

Robert to arrive." She shot a sharp glance at Hastings.

"My deepest apologies for that, once again," murmured Hastings in a suave voice. "But the ferry service is so erratic this time of year."

"Nothing today operates properly," Velma stated with a bored shrug. "You can't get decent service to save your life. Like that useless girl I hired. I don't suppose you're looking for a job as a companion, are you?" she asked Nancy.

"I'm afraid I'm already employed," Nancy replied quickly. She turned to Hastings. "May I use your phone to call a taxi?"

Hastings pointed to a phone on a small table in the hallway. The slim island phone directory lay beside it, and Nancy quickly looked up a cab company and dialed its number. While she made her call, Velma and Hastings talked quietly in the living room, but she couldn't hear what they said.

Returning to the living room, Nancy thanked Hastings. "This is a lovely house," she added cautiously. "Is it yours?"

"I'm renting it," he said coldly. "I needed a place to screen movies privately." Almost as an afterthought, he added, "I don't like spending my spare time around crowds of film people. They drive me crazy." What a statement, coming from a man who ran his own film festival! Nancy thought.

"What films have you been screening?" she asked, prepared to hear a lie.

Velma spoke up. "Robert has been kind enough to invite me to speak at his festival," she said blithely. "He asked me here today to watch a new print of one of my old films, which he has cleverly managed to get hold of." She paused.

Was Velma going to spill the truth? Nancy watched Hastings's face carefully, waiting for him to explode.

Then Velma continued, "Of course, it's not one of my favorites, since Joseph Block did not direct it."

Not a Joseph Block film? Nancy's heart sank with disappointment. Then this wasn't one of the stolen movies—all three of them had been by Block. Back to square one, she thought wearily.

A honk outside told them that the cab had arrived. Nancy hurried over to help Velma out of her chair and to the front door. Hastings followed behind, thanking Velma again and again.

Nancy helped Velma into the cab. As they pulled away from Hastings's house, Velma sighed. "What an absolute windbag that man is," she commented. "I swear, he'd say anything to advance the cause of his precious festival. If it weren't such a respected event, I'd never have consented to appear at it." She turned to gaze out the window. "This place looks so different now. I haven't been here for so many years, not since . . ." Her voice trailed off sadly.

Nancy said gently, "Since you worked here with Joseph Block?"

For a moment Velma was silent. When she spoke,

86

her voice was contorted with rage. Nancy wouldn't have believed that so much anger could come out of such a small frame.

"Joseph Block was a genius," Velma said, quivering with emotion. "He was extraordinary! Anyone who worked with him understood that. But the studio heads never appreciated that. They were blind, all of them!"

She stopped to catch her breath, then continued, "They ruined his pictures when they added sound. He would never have allowed it if he'd been alive—never. I warned Steven Forelli not to show that fraudulent version of *A Day in the Country*, but he wouldn't listen."

Nancy was alarmed when she saw how upset Velma was. As the taxi pulled up into the short line waiting for the ferry, Nancy did her best to calm her down. But Velma just stared trembling out the window, her eyes filled with tears.

At last the ferry arrived. As the few cars on it drove off onto Chappaquiddick, Nancy sat up in surprise.

Joan Staunton was driving one of the cars, and Bill Zeldin was sitting beside her! Joan was talking animatedly to Bill, gesturing fiercely.

What were they doing here? Had they come to see Robert Hastings? It seemed like too much of a coincidence that they would be on this tiny island for any other reason. Nancy stared out the rear window, watching the car disappear up the hill.

Her mind racing, Nancy considered how she

could get out of the cab and follow Joan and Bill. Surely the cab driver could get Velma safely back to the Lookout Inn by herself.

But when she turned back to face the elderly actress, Nancy gasped with surprise.

Velma Ford lay slumped beside her on the seat, her eyes shut, not breathing!

10

Lies and Alibis

Nancy loosened the collar of Velma Ford's dress and rubbed her wrists gently in an attempt to revive her. At first there was no response at all. The cab driver leaned over the back of his seat, concerned.

But after a few minutes, Velma's eyelids fluttered and she straightened up. "What happened?" she mumbled.

"You passed out," Nancy said as she helped Velma up into a more comfortable sitting position.

"Oh, not again," Velma said with a weary sigh. "This happens sometimes when my blood sugar gets low. I didn't eat any lunch—I was too excited. And it was such a stressful day. It's so hard to look at my old movies and remember the days that are no more." She smiled weakly, patting Nancy's hand. "Don't worry, dear, I'll be all right."

The cab driver leaned over and pulled a crumpled box of crackers from his glove compartment.

89

He handed it back to Velma. "Here, lady," he said kindly. "Eating something might help."

Velma looked gratefully at the cabbie and mumbled her thanks. She took a cracker out of the box and nibbled it as they drove up the ramp onto the tiny ferry.

As the ferry chugged back across the harbor to Edgartown, Velma stared silently out the taxi window. Nancy wondered what she could say to cheer up the elderly actress. She was beginning to like Velma, now that she seemed more human.

Nancy's thoughts turned to Joan and Bill driving off the ferry on Chappaquiddick. She still couldn't figure Bill out. What had he wanted to talk to her about this morning? Did he know whom the brass button belonged to?

When the cab pulled up at the Lookout Inn, Nancy helped Velma to her room, which was a suite on the ground floor. She waited with her until a doctor arrived. The doctor confirmed Velma's diagnosis—low blood sugar—and advised her to order lunch from room service.

Leaving Velma's room, Nancy suddenly felt lightheaded herself. She realized that she had missed lunch, too. The inn dining room was closed, so she headed outside to grab a sandwich.

As she got near the waterfront, she guiltily remembered the motorboat she'd left on Chappaquiddick. She soon found the boy she'd rented the boat from and gave him another twenty dollars to go fetch his boat himself. Then she stopped in a deli and bought a tuna hero.

Returning to the inn, Nancy remembered that she still had to check Velma's alibi for Friday night, when the first film was stolen. "Could I talk to you a minute?" she asked the desk clerk.

"Sure," he replied in a friendly voice. "Now's a good time. The madness starts around five, when new guests are checking in and everybody else comes back to change for dinner."

Nancy smiled. "Can you remember if Velma Ford was around here on Friday night?" she asked.

"Friday night," the clerk mused. "Velma Ford is that gorgeous old actress, right?"

Nancy nodded, thinking how much Velma would have appreciated the use of the word *gorgeous.* "Yes, that's right," she said. "Was she here?"

"Why do you want to know?" the clerk asked, suddenly cautious.

Nancy was ready with an excuse. "I'm trying to help her find a purple scarf she misplaced," she said, hoping he wouldn't repeat that to Velma. "She asked me to help her track her movements on Friday night, so I'm starting with you."

"I haven't seen the scarf," he said. "She was here until about eight o'clock. I remember, because she asked me to call a cab for her."

"What cab company?" asked Nancy.

"If you'll hold on a minute . . ." The clerk rummaged around on a shelf beneath the counter and came up holding a pink slip of paper. "Yes, here it is. It was the Friendly Taxi Company. The cab took her to the Savoy Café. That's a new jazz place, on the waterfront in Oak Bluffs. The cab came at eight o'clock Friday night." He looked triumphant, and Nancy couldn't help smiling.

"Thanks, you've been real helpful," she said.

"Think nothing of it," the clerk answered. "I like that old lady—she's a class act."

Nancy went up to her room. Sitting on the bed eating her sandwich, she looked up the Savoy Café in the local phone book. When she called, though, there was no answer. "They must not be open yet." She sighed and hung up. She decided to wait until that evening and go to the café herself, with Bess and George.

Still wondering what Bill had to tell her, she dialed his hotel room next, even though she knew he wouldn't be there. She left a message, apologizing for having missed their meeting that morning and suggesting that they set up another time.

Just as she hung up, Bess and George knocked on the door and she let them in. Bouncing down on her bed, they started chattering about Henry Block and watching him work.

"It's a shame you missed it, Nan," said George. "He's doing this film about a boy who is kidnapped and held for ransom by pirates. When he grows up, he becomes a pirate, too. It's going to be great!"

"Why was he at the wildlife sanctuary?" Nancy asked.

"He was checking out the swampy wetlands in the sanctuary," George answered. "It looks like a jungle island, in a weird way."

"He didn't mind our being there at all," Bess added. "He was really nice, in fact. He let us follow them around as they looked at different locations, and he even asked our advice about what a teenage audience likes."

"I got to talking to one of Henry's production assistants," George added. "He told me that Henry might have taken his yacht, the *Joseph B*, out toward Gay Head last night. He often takes late-night cruises, the guy says. Henry says it relaxes him. But he usually goes alone."

"That's interesting," Nancy said. "At least we know that he could have been the one sending the Morse Code." She paused to lick some tuna fish off her fingers. "Now let me fill you in on what's been happening around here."

She told them about her non-meeting with Bill, the false alarm at the festival offices, and her expedition to Chappaquiddick. When she finished, George said, "It sounds to me like Velma Ford had a strong motive for stealing *A Day in the Country*. After all, she's the one who didn't want it to be seen."

"I disagree," Bess said. "I think Robert Hastings is the villain here. I bet he stole the film just to get Velma to speak at his festival."

Nancy shook her head. "I think you're both wrong," she said. "Hastings is the most obvious suspect, but I'm beginning to think he didn't do it. I didn't see any of the stolen films at his beach house. And I can't believe he's the one who pushed me off the merry-go-round. He's such a big man that either Bill or that little boy would have identified him. Besides, he's so open about his dislike and jealousy of the Martha's Vineyard Film Festival. If you were trying to get away with something, wouldn't you keep quiet?"

"What about Velma?" George asked.

"I don't think Velma is capable of stealing the films. She's too frail to have managed it herself," Nancy said. "And she's such a private person, I don't think she would have planned the theft with someone else. She *is* angry at Steven Forelli for choosing to show the film with a soundtrack, but she punished him by refusing to speak. I don't think she'd have had the film stolen on top of that."

"Shouldn't you check out her alibi then?" George asked. "If you could prove she was somewhere else when the first movie was stolen, that would establish her innocence."

"That's exactly what I want to do," Nancy said. "The desk clerk here told me that Velma ordered a taxi at eight o'clock on Friday night to go to a jazz club in Oak Bluffs. Let's find out whether she was actually there. And maybe we could stay and hear some music. After all, we *are* here for fun."

"I'm glad to see you remember that!" Bess exclaimed, grinning.

* * *

It was a beautiful warm evening, and the girls dressed in jeans and light sweaters. As they pulled into the center of Oak Bluffs, George looked at her guidebook and said, "The Savoy Café is on the waterfront. Park as close to the wharf as you can."

They found a parking space near the pier where the ferries from the Cape docked. Several noisy gulls circled over their heads, on the lookout for food. As they headed across the street toward the Flying Horses carousel, George pointed to a small, brightly lit building on the corner, facing the harbor. "That must be it," she said. "I can hear a saxophone."

The café's open front door spilled light and noise out into the evening. They could hear the saxophone clearly now, accompanied by a piano, bass, and drums. As the girls entered the club, the song ended and the audience burst into applause.

A young woman approached them, wearing a black T-shirt with the words *Savoy Café* printed on it in white letters. "Can I help you?" she asked.

"Yes, we'd like a table, please," Nancy said. "That is, if there is one." The room was very crowded, and Nancy couldn't see an empty space anywhere.

"Oh, don't worry, we'll manage." The young woman led them to a tiny table with three chairs, far from the stage, and handed them menus. "If you want something to eat, just ask. I'm Gillian."

"Could I ask you a question?" Nancy said. "It's about Friday night."

"Friday?" Gillian said. "We had the Pharaoh Quartet that night. They were incredible."

"Did you notice an older woman come in alone?" Nancy asked. "She's very thin, about five feet four inches tall, with dark hair—not gray—piled on top of her head. She was probably dressed in colorful clothes, maybe a huge hat with a long black veil—"

"Velma Ford," Gillian said promptly. "Isn't she fabulous? Yeah, she was here for the eight-thirty set. Loved every minute of it, too. She even stayed for the second set."

"What time did she leave?" asked Nancy.

"She was here till at least eleven o'clock. What a character! I seated her right near the stage, right where those two guys are sitting, over there." Gillian pointed to a small table for two on the right side of the stage.

Nancy did a double take. Sitting at the table were Bill Zeldin and Robert Hastings, deep in conversation.

"Okay, thanks, Gillian," Nancy said. As Gillian left the table, Nancy turned to Bess and George. "Do you see what I see? Look over there—Bill and Robert Hastings."

"I wonder what they're talking about," George said.

"Well, there's one way to find out," Nancy said, standing up. "I need to talk to Bill anyway, to arrange another meeting. But first I'll have to get him away from Hastings. I'll be right back."

Nancy threaded her way among the tables. Candlelight cast shadows over the people's faces in the dimly lit room, and a buzz of conversation underlaid the pulsing music.

When she was halfway across the room, Bill lifted his head and caught sight of her. Muttering something to Hastings, he stood up abruptly and left the table, heading away from Nancy.

Before Nancy could catch up to him, Bill had slipped into the men's rest room near the stage. Puzzled, Nancy stood against the wall near the rest-room door, waiting for Bill. Several minutes passed, and he still didn't come out.

After fifteen minutes Nancy returned to her table, keeping an eye on the rest-room door in case Bill finally emerged. George and Bess had ordered sodas and were listening to the music.

"This just isn't my day," Nancy shouted above the music as she sat down. "Bill sure seems to be avoiding me."

"Maybe because he's guilty of something?" George suggested reluctantly.

Nancy shrugged. "Maybe. Or maybe he didn't want Hastings to see us together for some reason."

"Seems like everybody from the festival found out about this place," Bess commented. "While you were over there, Nancy, Henry Block came in, alone. Then Joan Staunton came in with some guy. We tried to keep an eye on Henry, but he kind of disappeared into the crush by the bar."

Nancy sipped her soda. Her mind still on the case, she stared absent-mindedly at the band as they played a slow version of a well-known jazz song.

Toying with her napkin, she suddenly realized that there was something written on it in red ink. Opening it up, she spread it on the table.

The message was written in capital letters. It said, "COME OUT TO THE ALLEY—ALONE. I KNOW WHO STOLE THE MOVIE."

11

Hidden in the Past

Nancy quickly showed the message on her napkin to Bess and George. They stared at it, confused. "Who could have left that?" George asked. "Bess and I were here the whole time."

"In this crowd, anyone could have gotten close enough to leave it while you guys were looking at the band or talking to Gillian," Nancy said. "The only way to find out is to do what it says—go out to the alley. And I'd better go alone," she added, silencing their protests.

"Okay," George said, looking skeptical, "but if you aren't back in ten minutes, we're coming out after you."

The cool night air outside felt wonderful after the hot, noisy room. Nancy walked around to the alley running alongside the building. The end of the alley came out onto the harbor. Nancy waited there, looking out to sea.

Suddenly she heard sea gulls quarreling and squawking, just above her head. At the same moment, she began to feel pelted with small bits of something soft. In an instant she was surrounded by screaming gulls, beating their wings around her head and pecking fiercely. She was being attacked.

Flailing at the gulls with both arms, Nancy beat her way out of the wild tangle of birds. She ran under the awning of the Savoy Café for safety. Reaching up with her hand, she discovered bits of soggy french fries caught in her hair. The hungry birds had obviously been drawn to the fries. "Yuck!" Nancy muttered, disgusted.

But it was no laughing matter. Her face and arms were scratched from the gulls' sharp beaks. She was relieved to see Bess and George walk out of the club. "What on earth happened to you?" Bess gasped.

"I'm not sure how it happened," Nancy said, her voice shaky, "but I was attacked by a flock of savage sea gulls! I know it sounds weird, but it's the truth. Someone dropped french fries on me from the roof, I think, and the birds went after them." She stepped out from under the awning and arched her neck, looking up at the top of the building. "I'd better check up there. Maybe the person who did this left a clue behind."

Nancy quickly found a fire escape leading up the side of the building to the roof. Bess and George climbed up right behind her. When they reached the top, they found a gull picking at a grease-stained red-and-white-checked cardboard container. George looked uneasy. "The Savoy Café serves their french fries in a dish like that," she said.

Nancy leaned over the edge of the roof to look at the crowded café entrance below. "We can ask the people at the door if they saw anyone climbing up the fire escape," she said. "But I think it's unlikely anyone would have noticed in that mob scene." She pulled the napkin from her pocket and examined the red printing. "It's written in block capital letters—the hardest writing to identify," she added. Shaking her head, she headed back to the fire escape.

The girls made a few inquiries, but no one at the café had noticed anything. And Bill Zeldin, Robert Hastings, and Henry Block had all left.

Back in her hotel room an hour later, Nancy dabbed at her scratches with cotton balls soaked in rubbing alcohol. Bess and George sat perched on her bed. "I bet Bill Zeldin set those gulls on you, Nancy," George declared. "His disappearing act in the club looks awfully fishy."

Bess shook her head. "Robert Hastings was there, too, remember. He could have done it just as easily as Bill could have," she pointed out.

"So was Henry Block," Nancy added. "From what you learned today, it looks like he may have been the one sending the Morse code last night on the beach. The part of the message I wrote down

101

was 'have shooting script, lie low for now.' Maybe that could tie in to the stolen films." She frowned, perplexed.

"Don't forget, Bill was on the beach. Maybe the message was being sent to him," George said. "I still think he's connected somehow."

Nancy winced as she spread alcohol on a deep scratch. "Ow! Well, at least there's one person we can rule out—Velma Ford," she said. "We didn't see her at the café, and I doubt she could have climbed up onto that roof."

"Great," Bess said wryly. "One suspect eliminated. We're really making progress."

"I just wish we'd been able to see *A Day in the Country* before it was stolen," Nancy fretted. "There could be some clue in the film itself. Maybe I could talk to Joan Staunton tomorrow. She's one of the few people around who has actually seen that movie. She also knows all about Joseph Block from writing his biography. Maybe something in his life story could crack this case open."

"It's funny," George mused. "Nobody watches silent movies anymore, except a few film buffs. But here are all these people getting worked up over Joseph Block's movies. Maybe there *is* something important about him we don't know. But the guy's been dead since 1929. How can we go back in the past to find out about him?"

"The Block family has a summer home on the Vineyard," Bess said. "I'll bet the local newspaper, the *Vineyard Tribune*, can tell us lots about them, Henry as well as Joseph."

"Excellent idea, Bess," Nancy said. "If you two go to the *Vineyard Tribune* office tomorrow morning and do some research, I'll interview Joan. And I still want to talk to Bill."

The next morning after breakfast, George and Bess drove off in the red rental car to Vineyard Haven, where the *Vineyard Tribune* office was. Nancy phoned Bill and then Joan, but neither was in. She left messages for both of them to call her. For an hour she waited impatiently in her hotel room. Then, unable to sit still any longer, she walked over to the Harbor House to look for them. The desk clerk told her that both Bill and Joan had gone out early that morning.

Nancy walked past the festival building, where the morning session had started twenty minutes earlier. The lobby and the ground-floor offices were silent and deserted.

Next she went down to the harbor to check out Henry Block's yacht. Moored to the pier, it bobbed gently in the water. No one was aboard.

Frustrated, Nancy returned to the Lookout Inn. She stood uncertainly in the lobby, thinking where to go next. Just then a waiter came out of a doorway in a small corridor just off the lobby. "Thank you very much, Miss Ford," he called out before he turned and shut the door.

Velma Ford's suite! Nancy thought. The actress was there right now. It was a perfect opportunity to question her about *A Day in the Country* and Joseph Block. Nancy marched over to the doorway and knocked.

"Come in!" called a bright voice from within.

Nancy pushed the door open. "I wanted to see how you were feeling today, Ms. Ford," she said.

Velma Ford, wearing a gaudy orange-and-yellow-print caftan, was sitting on a small balcony off the suite's cozy front parlor. Her breakfast lay on a tiny wrought-iron table beside her.

"How kind of you, dear," she said, perking up. She waved to Nancy to join her. "I must say, I was feeling a little blue today. Thinking about the past," she said as Nancy stepped onto the balcony. She lifted a long cigarette holder to her mouth. Nancy saw no cigarette in it.

Noticing Nancy's glance, Velma said, "Even now that I've given up smoking, I still have to have my cigarette holder. It's always been my trademark. Joseph Block gave it to me, you know."

Nancy admired the beautiful enamel holder. "Were you very close to Joseph Block?" she asked.

The actress's face quickly darkened. "I suppose you want to know the same thing everyone wants to know," she said bitterly. "'Why did you stop working?' they all ask. Well, I'll tell you why." She pointed brusquely at a chair and Nancy sat down.

"When I first met Joseph Block, I didn't know a thing about acting," Velma declared. "I thought

104

you just smiled into a camera and looked pretty. Joseph changed all that. He was the only director I knew who cared as much about actors as about the film. He taught me how to express emotion in front of a camera—anger, fear, pain, joy, everything."

The actress stopped and cleared her throat. When she continued, her voice was quiet. "After he died, I lost the desire to act," she said simply.

Nancy touched Velma's arm gently and said, "I understand how difficult his death must have been for you." She hesitated a moment before saying, "What was the last movie you made with him?"

"Something called *Soldier of Fortune*," Velma said. "It was finished, but the studio never released it. They wanted to add a soundtrack—those barbarians!—and Joseph wouldn't let them. We had just started a new picture, supposedly a sequel to *A Day in the Country*. Same cast, same location, everything. But we'd only shot a few scenes when . . . he died."

"What was the movie about?" Nancy asked.

"I don't know," Velma admitted. "Some directors in the old days gave scripts to their actors, complete with stage directions and dialogue. But usually Joseph didn't. He just told us what to say and do, and we did it. He had his shooting script, of course."

Nancy sat up straighter. The Morse code message the other night had mentioned a shooting script. "What's that?" she asked.

"It's the final script the director works from when

105

he's ready to shoot the film," Velma explained. "It's the only one he marks with his own notes. Joseph used to throw away his shooting scripts after the movies were made. On the pictures I made with him, I asked him to give me the shooting scripts— for posterity, you know. But I never read the script for that last picture. After he died, I just didn't have the heart. . . ." Her voice trailed off and she looked very sad.

"You were making the movie here on the Vineyard?" Nancy asked gently.

"Yes, we'd already shot three scenes in different locations," Velma recalled, sitting up and taking a sip of coffee. "One odd thing, though—the costumes we had on weren't right. *A Day in the Country* was set in the 1890s, but for the sequel, we just wore our own street clothes."

"Really?" Nancy asked, surprised.

"Yes," Velma said. "I remember, because I was wearing patent-leather high-heeled shoes, and the heels kept sinking into the mud at the graveyard. They were much too modern for the time period. Perhaps the sequel was supposed to be set thirty years later, but then why weren't the characters made up to look older? It was most peculiar."

"Ms. Ford, can you think of any reason why someone would steal three Joseph Block movies from the Martha's Vineyard Festival?" Nancy tried to lead the actress back to the subject.

Velma Ford shook her head. "Those pictures are

classics. There are copies of them in film libraries all over the country," she said. "This horrible sound version of *A Day in the Country* is a new print, I suppose, but the others were all the good old silent classics. Someone's trying to sabotage this festival, that's all."

Velma set down her coffee cup and rose to her feet. "And frankly, I don't care," she went on. "I'm leaving today. I was just about to pack."

Realizing that this was a signal for her to go, Nancy thanked the actress and said goodbye.

Returning to her room, Nancy called to check her phone messages. There was still no word from Joan or Bill. Nancy sat on her bed, chewing a fingernail. Then a knock came on the door, and she sprang up to open it. "Wow, Nancy, did we hit pay dirt!" Bess exclaimed, bustling into the room.

"In the old newspapers?" Nancy asked.

"We spent two hours staring into a microfilm viewer," George groaned, following Bess into the hotel room. "We're lucky the *Tribune* is only a weekly paper. Imagine how many rolls of microfilm it would take to cover seventy years of a daily newspaper!"

"This is what we learned from various articles," Bess said, taking out a sheet of notebook paper. "The Block family has been summering on the Vineyard since the 1920s, when Joseph Block first bought a house here."

"There was one weird article from 1929, just

before Joseph Block died," George said. "It reported the disappearance of Block's film *Soldier of Fortune* from Cameo Studios."

Nancy raised her eyebrows. "That was his last completed film. The studio never released it," she said.

"How did you know that?" George wondered.

"I talked to Velma Ford this morning," Nancy said. "I'll tell you about that. But go on."

"Apparently, Block was furious with the studio for tryin g to add a soundtrack," George said. Nancy nodded. That supported what Velma had told her. "They believed he stole the movie to prevent it from being released," George went on. "He was never formally charged, but the studio canceled his contract. Then he died soon afterward."

"We read his obituary, too," Bess said. "He was killed in a car accident on the Vineyard, but we already knew that. He's buried here, in the Chilmark Cemetery. His widow was named Margot, and his only child was a son, Henry. He was the grandfather of our Henry," she added.

"But get this," George went on. "At the time he died, Joseph had been in the middle of getting a divorce. And he was engaged to be married."

"To whom?" Nancy asked.

Bess couldn't contain herself anymore. "To Velma Ford!" she shouted gleefully.

12

A Missing Link

"Velma Ford was going to marry Joseph Block!"
Nancy exclaimed. "No wonder she's so protective
of his films! She was in love with him. Oh, I wish I'd
known that when I talked to her this morning."

"Maybe we should go see her now," Bess said.

Nancy hesitated. "I just left a few minutes ago,
and she was about to pack," she said. "I don't want
to be pushy—she could refuse to talk to me. We
can try after lunch. Besides, the morning session of
the festival is almost over. If we head over there
now, we might be able to find Joan or Bill."

Bess and George agreed. They left the hotel and
strolled through Edgartown to the theater.

When they got to the theater, the girls stood near
the front door to watch the crowd filing out. They
stood next to a large signboard, where photos from
various films being shown at the festival were
displayed.

109

Nancy and George craned their necks, scanning the crowd. "Hunh!" Bess said. "That's weird."

"What's weird, Bess?" Nancy asked.

"This picture," Bess replied, pointing to a large photo on the signboard. Nancy turned to look at it. It showed Velma and two other actresses walking arm in arm through a cemetery. "In these other pictures from *A Day in the Country,* the actresses have on long, old-fashioned dresses," Bess said. "But here they're wearing clothes from the 1920s. See the short skirts?"

Nancy peered at the photo. Her eyes darted down to check Velma Ford's shoes. She was wearing patent-leather high heels. "Velma told me about wearing those shoes," Nancy said slowly. "But she was talking about a *sequel* to this movie."

Bess frowned. "But the caption says this is from *A Day in the Country.*"

"The *new* version," Nancy pointed out. "I wonder . . . Joan Staunton said that ten minutes of newly discovered film had been added on to the end of *A Day in the Country.*"

"And she said that the studio restorers couldn't figure where those ten minutes fit into the movie," George noted.

"Right," Nancy said. "What if those ten minutes were never part of the movie to begin with? Maybe they were from the sequel! Velma told me that Joseph Block shot three scenes of it before he died."

"Wow," Bess said. "So this new version of *A Day*

110

in the Country actually contains the only surviving footage of that lost sequel! No wonder it's so valuable."

"But what if the studio has no idea how valuable it is?" George said.

Nancy's eyes narrowed. "I bet the studio doesn't know," she said. "But somebody else does. And that somebody must be our thief!"

The girls exchanged a long, solemn look.

"Let's see if Steven Forelli is in his office," Nancy suggested. "Perhaps he knows where this photo came from."

Nancy led the way to Forelli's office, where they found him at his desk. He looked up as he heard them enter.

"Oh, it's you," he said, sitting up and running his hand through his thinning hair. "It's been a terrible day," he confided. "Apparently, the films that were stolen yesterday were the only reprocessed prints of these movies. It would take the studio too long to make copies and get them here, so I have to cancel those two screenings. A lot of people will be screaming for their money back, no doubt. But I can't refund their money without going broke."

Nancy started to say something sympathetic, but Forelli held up his hand to silence her.

"Wait, it gets worse," he continued. "The studio is threatening to sue me for five million dollars if they don't get their films back." He looked despairingly around the office. "All of this will come to an end."

111

Nancy said, "I'm so sorry. I know it seems like you'll never get the films back. But maybe there's still hope." She paused, then asked, "The large photo in the middle of the signboard outside— where does it come from?"

Forelli looked confused. "Why, from *A Day in the Country*," he said. "Isn't it clearly marked?"

"But which part of *A Day in the Country* is it from?" Nancy persisted. "From the newly added ten minutes?"

Forelli thought for a moment. "Now that you mention it," he said finally, "I don't remember that scene from the original film. Of course, I saw that movie years ago, when I was still in film school. But you may be right."

"What time period is *A Day in the Country* set in?" Nancy asked.

"Definitely the 1890s," Forelli said. "It's a film about America changing from a land of farms to a nation of big cities. That change became apparent at the very end of the nineteenth century—"

"Thanks," Nancy interrupted him, before he could get going on his lecture. "But the actresses' clothes in the photo look like they're from the 1920s, don't they?"

Forelli looked upward, picturing the photo in his mind. "Hey, you're right!" he said. "Something about that picture always bugged me. It just didn't have the right period feel. But why is that so important?"

"The extra ten minutes of footage may have something to do with why the film was stolen," Nancy explained. "And if I can figure out why it was stolen, I'll be closer to figuring out who the thief was."

"Good luck," Steven Forelli said. "I certainly hope you're on the right track!"

As he said goodbye to the girls, his expression already looked a good deal happier, Nancy was glad that she could offer him some hope. Now if only I can figure out where this information leads me, she reflected.

"If we could see that film, it might explain a lot," Bess remarked as they walked outside the festival building. The crowd from that morning's screening had already dispersed.

"Great," George said. "Seeing the film might help us figure out why it was stolen, but we can't see it because it *was* stolen!"

Nancy checked her watch. "Let's go back to the inn and order lunch from room service," she suggested. "I'd like to try to talk to Velma before she leaves the island. And if I can, I'd also like to interview Joan Staunton. The possibility that Joseph Block stole *Soldier of Fortune* from Cameo Studios is very odd. Maybe Joan knows more about it."

"What about Bill?" George reminded Nancy as they headed back to their hotel. "You never did find out what he knows about that brass button. And you have to admit, Nancy, he's been avoiding you lately."

"Bill's too nice to have done all those things to Nancy," Bess protested. "He's not the type to knock her off a carousel or push her over a cliff or make sea gulls attack her."

"I would like to talk to Bill, too," Nancy said. "But somehow I think we need to concentrate more on that extra ten minutes of footage—the sequel that never got finished." She thought for a moment, as they turned onto a tree-shaded side street. "Velma said that there were no costumes, that the actors wore their own clothes. So it looked like the time period was thirty years later, but the actors weren't made up to look older. If this was supposed to be a sequel, it should have followed directly from the plot of *A Day in the Country*. So why didn't it?"

"How can we answer those questions, Nan?" George asked. "It happened so long ago."

"Velma is our key," Nancy said. "She may remember more than she realizes."

When they arrived at the Lookout Inn, Nancy stopped to check for messages at the front desk. There was one from Bill Zeldin, saying, "Urgent—I must talk to you. Don't call me, I'll call you."

"Finally, a message from Bill," Nancy said, showing the note to Bess and George. "But unfortunately, I'll have to wait for him to call." She sighed and stuck the pink slip into her pocket. "At least he still wants to talk to me."

114

"The only person I want to talk to right now is room service," Bess said. "I'm starving."

"Okay." Nancy laughed. "You guys go ahead to your room. Order me a seafood salad. I just want to stop by Velma's room first and make sure she doesn't leave before we talk to her."

Bess and George headed upstairs. Nancy walked over to the doorway to Velma Ford's suite.

Noticing that the door was ajar, she knocked softly. Leaning forward to listen for a response, she thought she heard a scuffling sound inside. She pushed open the door a few inches wider and stuck her head inside.

Heavy curtains had been drawn over the doors leading to the balcony. The front parlor was shadowy and dark. But Nancy was sure she saw a figure crouched behind a small sofa in a dark corner of the room.

A shaft of light fell into the room from the hallway behind Nancy. The intruder stood up and whirled around with an armful of clothing. Before Nancy could look at the person's face, the bundle of clothes was flung in her face.

Nancy fought to disentangle her head from Velma's long, billowing dresses. Drawing in a deep, frantic breath, she almost choked on a mouthful of filmy silk. She tried to run to where the figure had been, but her feet got twisted in a length of chiffon and she nearly fell.

A moment later Nancy pulled the last long skirt

away from her face. The parlor was empty. The curtain over the balcony door had been yanked aside, and the open balcony door was still swinging on its hinges. The intruder had escaped by racing through the parlor out onto the balcony.

Just then Velma opened the door from her bedroom into the parlor. She saw Nancy standing there, still tangled up in Velma's clothes. "What are you doing here?" she demanded, her voice quavering with suspicion.

"I think I've just scared off a burglar," Nancy replied. She quickly explained to the actress what had occurred.

"Thank goodness you're all right!" Velma said, immediately changing her tone of voice. She took both of Nancy's hands in her own. "You could have been hurt!"

"I'm fine," Nancy assured her. "He didn't seem to be violent, just after something, that's all. I'm pretty sure it was a man, from his height and shape." Nancy led the trembling actress to an armchair and helped her to sit down. "Do you have anything here that someone might want badly enough to steal?"

"No, no. I don't have any jewelry with me, and I don't keep money in my hotel room," Velma said. "I can't imagine what . . ." The actress's voice trailed off. Then she got up and crossed the room. Behind the sofa, an open suitcase lay on the floor. The intruder had obviously been hunting through it, for

116

half its contents were tossed out onto the carpet nearby.

Velma stooped down and rummaged through the suitcase. She stifled a little gasp and stood up, swaying slightly on her feet. Then she hurried over to another suitcase, set on a desk near the bedroom door.

"What are you looking for?" asked Nancy.

"A big black binder," Velma said tersely. "It had all the shooting scripts in it."

"The shooting scripts from the Joseph Block films you worked on?" Nancy asked. "You had them here with you?"

"I thought someone here might be interested in Joseph Block's notes," Velma explained. "Some film buff, perhaps. The other night, in fact, that young man . . ." She paused for a moment. "Joan Staunton's assistant—what's his name?"

"Bill Zeldin," Nancy replied, trying to sound casual.

"Zeldin, yes," Velma said. "This Staunton woman is writing a biography of Joseph, you know. It's about time someone did. Anyway, her young man came to ask me about some scenes from *A Day in the Country*, so I was looking at the binder then. It was definitely in that suitcase, I'm sure of it."

Becoming more and more agitated, Velma scurried back to the rifled suitcase. She plucked frantically at the garments lying on the floor, checking beneath them.

"You're sure the binder was here. You didn't lend it to someone or leave it somewhere?" Nancy asked.

"Of course I'm sure," said the actress. "All of Joseph Block's shooting scripts! I had them here, and now they're gone!"

13

Another Stolen Movie

"Why would anyone steal Joseph Block's old shooting scripts?" Velma asked despairingly.

"You said yourself that you'd brought the shooting scripts because film buffs might be interested,"
Nancy pointed out. "What if one of these film buffs
really wanted the scripts? Or one particular
script?" Nancy paused, then asked, "Was the
shooting script for the sequel there, too?"

"Of course," Velma answered. "Joseph left it in
my hotel room, the night he died in that car crash. I
would never have given it up."

"Maybe there was something in that shooting
script that somebody wanted," Nancy suggested.
"Let's think this out. That movie was never completed. Only the people who were there when it
was filmed know anything about it."

"All those people are dead now," Velma stated.
"I was the youngest of the cast and crew. I was only

119

twenty years old. Now I'm ancient"—she smiled wryly—"and everyone else is dead."

"I want you to tell me everything you remember about filming the sequel," Nancy said. "But first, can we get my friends Bess and George to join us? The more minds we have working on this, the better."

An hour later Nancy, Bess, and George sat with Velma on her balcony over the remains of their lunch. Velma had changed her plans, determined to stay on the Vineyard until her stolen scripts were recovered.

At Nancy's suggestion, Velma had called the police about the intruder in her room. Officer Garvey had come to inspect Velma's hotel room, but the intruder had left no traces. There was no sign of a break-in, even. It seemed he had come in through the balcony door, which Velma had neglected to lock. "It's not even a case of breaking and entering," Officer Garvey had said as she was leaving. "Not much we can do."

The girls were now ready to hear Velma's recollection of filming the sequel. "I'd best give you some of the background first," she told them. "That will help me to remember."

"That's fine," Nancy said. "Go ahead."

"It all started just after *The Jazz Singer* was such a big hit," Velma recalled. "'Talkies' were all the rage, and silent movies were dying at the box office."

"Something like that happened when the music industry started issuing CDs instead of record albums," Nancy said. "My dad has lots of his favorite music on old records. But now you can't buy records anymore. Everything is released only on CDs."

"The world is just crazy for new technology," Velma said with a sigh. "Anyway, *A Day in the Country* had been doing well, but Cameo decided to withdraw it from the movie houses. The head of production at Cameo took Joseph's film, tacked on a soundtrack, and rereleased it. Of course Joseph was angry. Then he got depressed. I was worried and frightened."

"It must have been awful," Bess murmured.

"Joseph was right, you know," Velma said. "*A Day in the Country* was a flop when they added the soundtrack. But the studio paid no attention. *Soldier of Fortune* was almost finished at that point, and Joseph was so proud of it. He kept saying it was his masterpiece. Then they started telling him they wanted to add a soundtrack to that, too. He went into a rage."

"And then *Soldier of Fortune* disappeared," Nancy said, prodding the actress's memory.

Velma nodded. "I didn't dare ask Joseph about it. He'd have these furious fits. One morning he ripped the entire newspaper to shreds because of a silly gossip column about the studio's plans."

"Do *you* think he stole the movie?" Nancy asked.

Velma dropped her eyes. "Well, yes," she admitted in a small voice. "I thought he might have taken it and hidden it somewhere." She looked up with a flash of spunk. "Legally it was Cameo's, but it was really his work. I didn't know for sure what Joseph had done, though, and I couldn't ask him, he was acting so strange."

"When did he return to the Vineyard to make the sequel to *A Day in the Country?*" asked Nancy.

"Right after *Soldier of Fortune* disappeared," said the actress. "We arrived on the Vineyard, and that very day the police showed up. They questioned all of us for hours: Did we have any idea what Joseph might have done with the movie, questions like that. No one knew anything, of course. But it was upsetting and exhausting."

"And *Soldier of Fortune* was never recovered?" Nancy asked.

Velma shook her head. "After Joseph died, all his belongings went to his wife, Margot, even though they'd been separated for nearly a year." A bitter tone crept into Velma's voice. "I know *Soldier of Fortune* wasn't among his things. Margot had the nerve to call me late one night, asking where it was. I told her I had no idea; and even if I did, she'd be the last person I'd tell."

Nancy sat quietly, trying to piece together the information Velma had given her. Increasingly, this long-ago theft seemed connected somehow to the recent crimes. *Soldier of Fortune* had been stolen just before the sequel was shot. What had happened to that movie so many years ago?

Suddenly George spoke up. "A newspaper article

122

I read said that Cameo Studios canceled Joseph Block's contract after they thought he'd stolen *Soldier of Fortune*," she mentioned.

Velma looked surprised. "They did?" she said. "I assumed he was making the sequel for Cameo. In the old Hollywood days, everyone was under contract to one studio or another. All of Joseph's regular actors were under contract to Cameo. If Cameo had canceled his contract, they would never have let us work with him."

A silence fell upon the table. Velma looked at each of the girls, her large green eyes growing even wider. "Do you think he hid the fact that his contract was canceled just to get us up here to make that movie?" she asked.

Nancy raised her eyebrows. "But surely someone would have found him out," she reasoned. "Pretty soon the studio would have wondered where all these actors and technical people had gone. He could never have finished the movie."

Velma stared down at the table. "Maybe there was no movie to make," she said slowly. "We had no costumes, and there were no sets, really, since we were filming on location. Joseph could have paid for our travel expenses to get here. The cameramen just brought their equipment with them. Maybe the studio didn't know what he was doing."

"Why would he shoot a movie that could never be finished?" Bess asked.

Nancy's mind was racing. "Joseph wrote a script for a sequel," she said, "but we don't know if that's what he was filming up here. You said yourself, Velma, that those scenes seemed to have nothing to do with *A Day in the Country*. What if he was filming something entirely different?"

"Maybe it had something to do with *Soldier of Fortune*," George put in. "The police were after him. Maybe it gave him an alibi."

"Or maybe . . ." Nancy thought carefully. "Imagine you have something important you want to hide for a long time. But you want to make sure it can be found eventually, even if you're not around anymore. What do you do?"

"You leave a map," Bess said.

"No," Nancy said, "anyone could read the map, and it wouldn't stay secret for long. I think you would create a set of clues that only one or two people could interpret—people you trust."

Velma looked at Nancy intently. "Are you saying that Joseph used this short film as a set of clues to where he hid *Soldier of Fortune?*"

"Yes," Nancy said excitedly, "that's exactly what I'm saying!"

Velma slapped her hand down on the table. "That would have been just like Joseph," she declared. "He cared so much about what future generations would think of his movies. If he did steal that movie, he would have preserved it for future generations. He couldn't leave it to his son—Margot had poisoned the boy's mind against Joseph. So he left a set of clues to make sure some film lover would find it! He knew the studio would hang on to any film he shot, of course."

"It got tacked on to the end of *A Day in the Country* only by accident," Nancy noted. "Someone else figured this all out too, though. That's why *A Day in the Country* was stolen. It's the only place those clues have survived."

"The only place, except for Velma's mind," Bess added firmly.

"The discovery of a new Joseph Block film would be an astonishing find," Velma said. "And Joseph considered it his masterpiece. The studio would probably pay scads of money for its return. Or, of course, a scoundrel could make a fortune by selling it to a collector. Original films are like original works of art—they are worth the moon."

Nancy tried to stay calm. "He shot three different scenes, in three different locations," she noted. "The locations could be the clues. Do you remember where they were, Velma?"

"I can try," Velma replied. "My memory isn't so reliable about recent things, but I never forget anything about the past." The actress got up and slowly paced around the balcony.

Suddenly she stopped and threw her arms open wide. "I remember the first shot!" she declared. "It was at an old sea captain's house, outside of Edgartown. Maybe five miles away, though I can't be sure. Cars traveled slower then, so it took longer to get places."

"What else do you remember about this house?" Nancy asked intently. "There are lots of sea captains' houses on the Vineyard."

"Well," Velma said slowly, "this one was very old. And the man who owned it had made a famous sea voyage." She paused, then said triumphantly, "Yes! He sailed around the world alone."

"Great!" Nancy said. "George, check your guidebook. I'm sure it will mention this house. Then we can drive there and take a look. Do you mind going, Ms. Ford?"

"Mind? I insist! Let's go!" Velma Ford wheeled around and hurried back into her hotel room to grab a shawl. Nancy was amazed at the change in her. The age and frailness had fallen off, and she had become vital and energetic.

Nancy, Bess, and George hurried upstairs and picked up sweaters, purses, and car keys. A few minutes later, the four of them met in the lobby and headed out to the girls' rental car.

Nancy drove, with George beside her, guidebook in her lap. Velma and Bess sat in the back.

George was trying to find the captain's house that Velma had mentioned. "You said it was outside of Edgartown," George said. "In which direction?"

"All I know is that it was on the way to some other little town," Velma said hesitantly. "Maybe something with the word *West* in it."

"West Tisbury?" asked George. "Nancy, try taking the Edgartown Road toward West Tisbury." She continued to pore over the book. "Hey, what about the Joshua Slocum House? It says here that Captain Joshua Slocum made a successful around-the-world trip on his thirty-six-foot sloop *Spray*. In 1907 he tried another solo voyage around the world, but he was lost at sea."

"I think that's it!" Velma cried from the backseat. She leaned forward eagerly, staring out at the road ahead. "I'll know it when I see it."

George said to Nancy, "It'll be on your left, Nan, just after the youth hostel." She looked at her watch and added, "It's not quite five o'clock yet. It should still be open."

As they rounded a curve in the road, Velma shouted, "There it is!" Nancy pulled over and parked off the road beside a small single-story house with a sagging roof. The salty air had weathered the wood from brown to a mottled gray. A light was on inside, and the door stood open.

As they walked in, a middle-aged woman was tidying up. "We're closing in five minutes," she announced. "But you can take a quick look around."

Velma walked over to the fireplace and picked up a book propped open on the mantel. "It's the same book that was here all those years ago," she murmured. "It's as if time has stood still."

The attendant said in a friendly voice, "That book's been here at least as long as I have, which is about twenty-five years. It's part of the Vineyard Museum's collection."

Nancy looked at the title page: *Sailing Alone*

Around the World, by Captain Joshua Slocum. Velma looked over her shoulder and said, "That's what he filmed. Joseph made me open the book so he could get a shot of that front page."

The page contained a drawing of Slocum's sailing ship. Nancy asked excitedly, "Was there anything else he had you do while you were here?"

"No," said the actress. "That was all."

"I guess we need to see some of the other locations for this one to make sense as a clue," Nancy said. Thanking the attendant, they filed out of the house and got back in the car. "What was the next site?" Nancy asked Velma.

The actress leaned her head back and closed her eyes. "It was another place along here somewhere," she recalled vaguely. "I remember we didn't drive very far, and our driver commented that we could have walked." She opened her eyes with a self-mocking grin. "Isn't it strange the things one remembers?"

Nancy began to drive slowly along the Edgartown Road. Twenty minutes later Velma frowned. "It wasn't this far, I'm sure," she said. "It wasn't a house or anything, just a spot by the side of the road. There was a pile of stones there or something."

As Nancy turned the car around, George began to flip through the guidebook, tilting it closer to the window to catch the dying light of early evening. "There are a few historic markers along this road," she muttered. "Uh, hold on, could this be it? 'The

Place on the Wayside, four and a half miles from Edgartown,'" she read. "'It's a stone marker in memory of Thomas Mayhew Jr., who preached to the Native Americans on this spot. They placed stones here as a sign of their affection. The pile of stones grew over the years, and now they've been cemented together.' It's a little distance down this way, Nan."

"Okay," Nancy said. "Keep your eyes open, Velma, and shout if you see it." She drove down the road at a slow crawl.

Suddenly everyone in the car shouted, "Stop!"

"I see it, I see it!" Nancy said with a laugh. She steered the car over to the side of the road, right by a small patch of trees.

Just then a large dark car hurtled over the rise behind them. Before they realized what was happening, the car was swerving sharply to the side, heading right for them!

14

The Trail Leads to Danger

The dark car screeched up behind the red rental car and rammed it from the rear. The red car jolted forward and slid onto the steep gravel shoulder of the road. The dark car turned sharply and roared away, melting into the gathering darkness along the Edgartown Road.

Nancy desperately tried to steer away from the roadside ditch. She'd had no time to study the dark car's make, let alone the license-plate number or the face of the driver. Once the danger was past, Nancy asked if anyone else in the car had seen anything. George, Bess, and Velma all said it had happened too quickly for them to have seen anything.

Nancy climbed out to check the car. George joined her, while Velma and Bess stayed inside. The right rear taillight was broken, but other than that there was no damage.

"You think it was deliberate?" George asked.

Nancy nodded grimly. "It was deliberate, all right," she said. "But who did this? That's what I'd like to know."

George walked over to the monument. "Well, here's the Thomas Mayhew marker. For what it's worth, we've found the second location. I don't see anything special about it, do you?"

"Maybe it's not the marker itself that's important," Nancy mused. "It could be a symbol for something else or a verbal clue. Stone, Indian, roadside . . . one of those words might mean something once we see the whole pattern."

They got back in the car. "Well, was that enough excitement for you?" Bess was asking Velma, trying to make light of their near accident.

Velma said, "You know, I thought someone was following us. I saw that car back at the Joshua Slocum House. It stopped when we stopped, but the driver didn't get out. And then when we left, that car started up again."

"Did you see who was driving?" Nancy asked, mentally chiding herself for not having noticed the car herself.

"No," Velma admitted. "All I could see was that there was only one person in it."

"Was it a man or a woman?" asked Nancy.

"I couldn't say," Velma replied. "The way young people dress today, you all look the same to me."

Nancy exchanged a smile with George and Bess.

She started the car. "Okay," she said to Velma, "can you remember the next location?"

"Yes, this one I remember well," said the actress. "It was the Chilmark Cemetery."

"That's on South Road," George said. "I looked it up earlier, because that's where—" She stopped abruptly.

"Where Joseph Block is buried," Velma said, calmly finishing George's sentence. "Of course I know that, girls. I've never been there before. Margot wouldn't let me near the funeral, and afterward I couldn't bear to visit his grave on my own. But now I actually think I'd like to see it. It's time at last."

Nancy put the car in gear, and they headed along Edgartown Road until it intersected with South Road. She turned left, knowing that the road ran through Chilmark on the way to Gay Head.

As she drove, Nancy kept her eyes open for the car that had hit them, but she didn't see it. If someone was following them, he or she was doing it very discreetly, she thought to herself.

The winding road became more hilly as they approached the cemetery. They parked and got out of the car. It was fully dark now, but they could still see beautiful trees and flowering bushes. The graves were spaced well apart from one another, giving a sense of peace and privacy. Nancy took her penlight from her purse and began to flash it over the rows of headstones.

"When Block filmed you here, were you standing in a specific place?" Nancy asked Velma.

"I can't remember," Velma admitted. "When we got here, it had just started to rain. I was anxious to finish shooting, because it had been a long day. But Joseph insisted that we continue."

Nancy followed Velma around, reading the headstones. They came across Joseph Block's grave under a large old oak tree. "He always loved this place, with its view of the ocean and the marshes," Velma said. She looked around, then said sadly, "The pines have grown so tall. I bet they block the view now. What a shame."

She stooped down by the grave and ran her fingers over the cold headstone. "And he loved the old Indian cemetery with its stone markers." She stopped abruptly, then turned around and pointed. "That's where he filmed us! He took us into the Indian cemetery—just beyond that gate!"

Gesturing for the girls to follow, Velma led them into the older part of the cemetery. It had been used by the Native Americans on the Vineyard before the settlers moved in, she explained. Taking the penlight from Nancy, she moved from stone to stone, examining each one carefully.

"What are you looking for?" asked Nancy.

"We were filmed standing by an old headstone, really old and cracked," Velma said. "And it said something strange on it."

"What exactly do you mean by 'strange'?"

George asked, trying to read the epitaph on another headstone in the pale moonlight.

"I'll know it when I see it," Velma said. They all joined in the hunt, reading out epitaphs that struck them as unusual.

Suddenly Nancy read out in a clear voice, " 'Step into the light.' "

"What did you say?" Velma asked. She wheeled around, flashing the penlight toward Nancy. "Say that again!"

" 'Step into the light,' " Nancy repeated.

"That's it!" Velma cried. "That's the stone he had me pose in front of." She hurried over to Nancy, who stood bent over a small, crude headstone. Velma trained the narrow beam of the flashlight on the stone. The carving had almost disappeared, but the words were still readable: "Step into the light."

The girls and Velma stood quietly for a moment, fixing the whole scene around the grave in their minds. Then Nancy said, "Let's get back into the car. It's getting chilly out here." They headed back to the parking lot.

"So where do we go now?" Bess asked, stumbling as she crossed the shadowy graveyard. "Are there any more locations?"

"No, this was the last place," Velma said. "There were only three, and you've seen them all."

"I still don't see how these locations add up to clues," George grumbled.

They all fell silent for a moment, racking their brains to solve Joseph Block's baffling riddle. As they reached the car, Bess spoke up. "You know," she offered, "the Thomas Mayhew monument and the cemetery both have to do with Native Americans. Could that be a connection?"

"Good thinking, Bess," said Nancy. "Velma, was *Soldier of Fortune* a movie about Indians?"

Velma shook her head. "No, it was set during the First World War," she said.

Everyone climbed into the car, still thinking. "The Joshua Slocum House doesn't have a Native American connection," George noted. "It had to do with sailing ships and a book about a sea voyage."

Nancy slipped her key in the ignition, but she didn't start the car yet. "What about the headstone?" she mused. "How would that tie in?"

"'Step into the light,'" George murmured. "I guess it means the light of heaven, but in my mind I see an old-fashioned lamppost or a lantern."

"It was on an Indian headstone," Bess reminded them. "I guess most of the Native Americans who lived at Gay Head were buried here."

"Gay Head?" Nancy repeated. Then an idea went off in her head. "That's it! Gay Head was a Native American settlement, right? And it has a lighthouse—as in 'Step into the light.' A lighthouse would have helped sea captains—like Joshua Slocum—on their voyages. *Soldier of Fortune* must be hidden at the Gay Head lighthouse!"

"Nancy, that's brilliant!" cried Bess.

In her dramatic voice, Velma added, "Congratulations, Miss Drew, I do believe you've cracked it."

Quivering with excitement, Nancy switched on the car, threw it into reverse, and backed out of the parking lot. "George, tell me how to get to Gay Head from here."

As they raced along the South Road, they talked about where the film might be hidden in the lighthouse. "Let me look up the lighthouse," George said, pulling out the guidebook and shining Nancy's penlight on the pages. She started reading. "'The original wooden lighthouse was one of the first revolving ones in the country. In 1856 it was replaced by a larger steel design that contained a stronger light with a special lens. In 1952 an automatic light was constructed, and the old lens was given to the Vineyard Museum.'"

"Oh, no!" Bess said in dismay. "What if Joseph Block hid the film somewhere in the old lens mechanism? Does this mean it was removed when the lens was replaced in 1952?"

Everyone was silent for a moment as they considered this possibility. Finally, Nancy said, "Well, all we can do is look. If it's not there, maybe that *is* what happened. Then we'll have to rethink the whole thing."

As they pulled into the center of Gay Head, the lighthouse loomed ahead, near the top of the cliff. The big light at the top sent out alternating beams of red and white light.

"Look at that!" whispered Nancy, pointing at the top of the lighthouse as she pulled into the parking lot. Below the big beams, they could spot a smaller

136

white light, moving from one window to another in the lighthouse tower. "Someone's looking for something up there with a flashlight," Nancy said uneasily.

She looked around to study the parking lot. In it she could spot a large, dark car similar to the one that had tried to hit them.

Shifting her car into park, Nancy opened her door. "Bess, take over the wheel," she ordered. "Drive with Velma up to the Clifftop Restaurant and call the police for backup. Ask for Officer Poole. George, I'll need you to stay outside the lighthouse to act as a lookout."

George said reluctantly, "Okay, but if anything happens, just yell and I'll come running. This could be dangerous."

Nancy and George hopped out of the car. Bess slid into the front seat and drove quietly away.

While George tucked herself behind a clump of beach plums, Nancy went to the front door of the lighthouse and edged quietly in. A spiral staircase wound up the inside of the tower. Nancy crept up the steps, making as little noise as possible.

But as she rounded the last curve, she gasped with surprise.

Glaring down at her from the top of the stairs was Joan Staunton. And in one hand she brandished a large iron bar.

15

Step into the Light

Nancy thought fast. I've got to distract her, she realized. "Joan!" she said brightly. "I can't believe you figured this puzzle out before I did. I'm impressed."

"I wasn't trying to impress you," Joan snarled. "I've been working on this for a long time. Now that it's about to pay off, no one can take it away from me—not Joseph Block's relatives, not my interfering secretary, and certainly not a girl detective." She raised the iron bar over her head threateningly and took a step toward Nancy.

Nancy started to inch backward down the stairs. "Don't try to get away!" Joan ordered.

Suddenly, with a loud *Argh!* Bill Zeldin shot out of the shadows behind Joan. He hurled his shoulder into her knees, knocking her to the floor. Grabbing the wrist of the hand that held the iron

138

bar, he forced her to drop it. The bar flew against a wall with a loud clank.

Joan kicked and screamed and struggled, but between Bill and Nancy, she didn't have a chance. While Bill pinned her down, Nancy swiftly tied Joan's wrists and ankles with a couple of elastic cords Bill had brought. "You certainly came prepared for battle," Nancy grunted to Bill.

"Where'd you come from?" Joan snarled at Bill.

"Before you came into the lighthouse, while you were hunting around the base of the tower, I slipped inside," Bill told Joan. "I climbed to the top and watched you from the tower window. When you finally came in, I hid behind the door to the storage closet, in the corner." He pointed behind them, where a door still stood open.

He turned to Nancy. "I owe you one," he added. "She was just about to discover *me* when she heard you climbing the steps. You were the distraction I needed to sneak up on her."

"Well then, we're even," Nancy said. "You saved me from quite a bashing."

"You little creep," Joan spat at Bill. "All that overtime you put in—you were just spying on me, weren't you?"

Bill sat back on his heels, grinning proudly. "I've been following you for days now," he explained. "I had a pretty good idea what you were up to. That's why I brought those from my bike." He pointed to the elastic cords, checking again to make sure they were tied securely.

"By the way," Bill told Nancy, "she didn't find the film. She looked around the base of the tower, and she explored just about every inch inside. It must not be here after all."

"Let's go downstairs and start all over again," Nancy said, persisting. "It has to be here somewhere." Glancing back at Joan, she added, "I guess it's okay to leave her here for now."

"I don't think she'll get very far," Bill said with a lopsided grin.

Bill and Nancy clattered down the winding metal staircase. Just as they walked out the door, Nancy stopped in the doorway. "'*Step* into the light,'" she said. "That's it! *Step.*"

She and Bill both looked down at the same time. Nancy was standing on the front step leading into the lighthouse. Bill's eyes lit up. "Eureka!" he exclaimed.

Suddenly a voice called, "Bill!" Taken off guard, Nancy spun around to see Henry Block appear out of the shadows at the side of the lighthouse.

"Henry!" Nancy said, confused.

Bill grinned. "He met me here on his yacht. It was the only way to get here faster than Joan." Seeing Nancy's puzzled expression, Bill added, "Henry and I became friends while I was helping Joan research her book about Joseph Block. When I realized she was doing something underhanded, I asked him to help me catch her."

"I went back to the boat to get these," Henry

said, holding up a claw hammer and a screwdriver. "When did you get here?" he asked Nancy.

Just then George came sprinting around the base of the lighthouse. She halted tensely when she saw Bill and Henry. Nancy waved to George. "It's okay, they're on our side," she said.

The four of them gathered around the doorstep, with Nancy quickly filling in George on the latest developments. Bending down, Henry used the screwdriver to pry up the stone. Nancy then took the claw end of the hammer and scraped at the soil beneath the step, while Henry dug with the screwdriver. "Remind me to carry a shovel around on my boat from now on," Henry muttered.

It was hard work, but after a few minutes Nancy finally saw something gleaming in the dark. It was the edge of an old metal trunk.

With a shout, they all fell on the trunk, clawing away at the earth that clung to it. Finally, Henry and Bill lifted it out of the hole.

"Buried treasure!" Henry cried. Placing the tip of the screwdriver against the lock, he banged it with the hammer until it broke open.

Nancy lifted the lid of the trunk. Inside they could see four old film cans, rusty but intact, clearly labeled *Soldier of Fortune*, 1929.

Just then they heard a siren wail up the road, heading toward them. A police car drove into view, its lights flashing. It pulled up to the lighthouse, followed by Bess and Velma in the red rental car. "I think you'll find someone you've been looking for inside," said Nancy to Officer Poole as he jumped out of his patrol car.

Officer Poole went in to take charge of Joan, while Officer Garvey, Bess, and Velma joined the small crowd standing around the trunk.

Tears welled in Velma's eyes as she read the label on the film cans. "After all these years," she murmured.

As Joan came out of the tower, led by Officer Poole, she shot a deadly look at Bill and came to a stop. "How did you know what I was doing?" she demanded.

"It wasn't so hard," Bill replied. "When you were reading Joseph Block's notes and diaries, I read them, too. Did you really think you were the only one smart enough to piece together what he wrote there?" He paused, then added, "I also know how greedy you are. I've seen you give films a rave review just because the producers promised you a little something on the side." Joan gasped, and Bill said quickly, "Don't deny it, Joan."

She turned away in a huff, but Bill pressed on. "I knew you'd pursue anything that might bring you fame and fortune," he said. "A long-lost Joseph Block masterpiece was too good to resist. When the projection room exploded at the screening Friday night, I was sure you weren't in the ladies' room as you said. So I started to follow you, to find out what you were up to."

Joan was enraged. "Of all the ungrateful— This is the last time I ever hire a male secretary!"

Officer Poole opened the patrol-car door and gestured for her to get in. "I think it may be a while before you hire anyone again," he said.

Bill nodded at the metal trunk containing the film cans. "I think this will be safer at the police station for now, don't you?" he asked the assembled group. They all agreed. He helped Poole put it in the trunk of the squad car.

The officers drove off for the state police station in Oak Bluffs. The girls and Velma piled back into their car, while Henry and Bill hiked back to the yacht. They all headed back to Edgartown, while the lighthouse went on flashing its red and white beams out over the dark cold ocean.

The next afternoon Nancy stood in the lobby of the festival theater with Bess, George, Velma Ford, Henry Block, and Bill Zeldin. "This is a great day," Velma Ford said, her eyes sparkling. "I owe you all so much."

Bess glanced around the crowded lobby. "It looks like most of the people who came for the festival are still here," she said. "I bet they're glad now that they didn't leave. They'll be the first audience anywhere to see *Soldier of Fortune!* It's amazing that, after all those years, it was still in good enough condition to show."

"Too bad Joan can't see it," Bill said wryly. "After all she went through to find it."

"What was she planning to do with *Soldier of Fortune* if she found it? Sell it?" George asked.

Bill shrugged. "More than anything, I think she wanted to create publicity for her biography of Block," he said. "It would have been a guaranteed bestseller. She was dying to be famous. And she really got obsessed with this."

Bill stopped to slip his knapsack off one shoulder. "Now that I have you here, Ms. Ford, I've got something of yours." He reached inside and pulled out a thick black three-ring binder.

Velma gasped. "Joseph's shooting scripts!" she exclaimed. "So *you* had them all the time."

Bill placed the binder in her hands. "That day I interviewed you, I sneaked the binder away with me," he admitted. "I was trying to return it when Nancy caught me in your room. I left with it still in my pack. I'm so sorry, but I needed to find out what those three scenes were all about."

"Did you find out?" Velma asked.

Bill shook his head. "Those scenes weren't even in the script for the sequel to *A Day in the Country*. But there was one thing—a handwritten note from Joseph Block." He leaned over and opened the binder to a page at the back.

Velma followed Bill's pointing finger. " 'Velma, my love,' " she read in a voice shaky with emotion. " 'The three extra scenes hold the key. Don't let *Soldier* be lost forever.' " She looked up, blinking away tears. "If only I'd had the nerve to read this

144

script before today," she said, "I could have found *Soldier of Fortune* years ago."

"Maybe and maybe not," Henry remarked. "You might not have been able to figure it out until Nancy Drew was around to help you."

Nancy shook her head modestly. "Joan figured it out on her own," she pointed out.

"Not entirely," Bill said. "Joan slipped off to Hastings's beach house late Sunday night to screen the stolen version of *A Day in the Country*. But apparently she still couldn't figure out the clues she saw in the film. So she had to follow you last night, Nancy, to see what you came up with. I guess she worked it out herself right before you did, because she got to the lighthouse sooner. And I was trying to follow her on my bike! Luckily there's a good bike trail cutting through the woods along Edgartown Road."

"Why didn't you tell me your suspicions about Joan?" Nancy asked.

"I didn't know you were a detective," Bill explained. "Then, after you fell off the carousel, I wondered why Joan was after you."

"So it was her brass button we found there!" Bess declared. "I *thought* you recognized it."

Bill shook his head. "Not at first," he said. "But that afternoon I noticed the buttons on a blazer Joan was wearing. When I realized she was the one at the carousel, I knew she was trying to scare Nancy off. I tried to warn you, Nancy, but I could never get you alone. Joan showed up at the beach that night—"

"And pushed me off the cliffs a few minutes later," Nancy added ruefully.

"She was hanging around at the top of the cliffs when I rode away on my bike that night," Bill admitted, "but I couldn't figure out why. Later, when I heard you'd been pushed over the cliffs, I realized how obsessed Joan was. I wanted to warn you, but you and I missed each other at the boat shed Sunday morning.

"Joan was getting so suspicious of me," Bill went on, "it was hard to get away. I saw you at the Savoy Café Sunday night, but both Joan and Robert Hastings were there. I actually thought they were in it together at that point."

"Joan must have set up that sea gull attack outside the café that night," said George.

"I didn't know about that one," Bill said, and George filled him in.

"It must have been Joan up on the roof," Bill said. "Hastings was inside the whole time. He wasn't involved at all, it turns out."

"I guess he really did cut his hand on a glass Sunday morning, just as he said he did," Nancy said. "And I was so sure he had set off the fire alarm at the festival office."

"No, that was Joan again," Henry said. "She stole the other two Block films, to divert attention from the theft of *A Day in the Country*. The police found all three films in a locker at the Vineyard Airport.

She had the locker key on her when they arrested her."

Nancy turned to Henry. "Was it you out in that boat Saturday night, sending Morse code?"

He smiled. "Yes, that was me."

"Why didn't you just use the phone?" George asked with a skeptical look.

Bill looked sheepish. "Well, I'd found Joan snooping around my desk and going through my phone messages, and I was getting nervous. So Henry and I arranged to use the code that night. I told Henry I had the shooting script. He said he understood that I had it and advised me not to do anything else until we spoke further."

"And that round package you were carrying the night of the theft?" Nancy asked Henry. "That really was one of your own films?"

"Yes," Henry said, smiling at Nancy. "I would have told you if you'd asked me."

George asked, "Why didn't you and Bill go to the police with what you knew?"

Henry answered, "I wanted to keep control of *Soldier of Fortune* until I could be sure Cameo wouldn't add a soundtrack to it. This morning I told the head of the studio that if they tried to add sound now, I would tell every major newspaper in the country. There would be mountains of bad publicity. He agreed real fast," he finished, grinning.

Steven Forelli approached them, smiling and rubbing his hands together. "This is a great day, indeed," he said. "The studio canceled its lawsuit, since we recovered all of the missing Block films, plus a lost masterpiece! And now the festival can really get under way."

The bell rang, signaling the start of the screening. The crowd in the lobby started filing into the theater. "There's something I haven't told you," Bill said to Nancy as they walked in. "Henry and I have decided to collaborate on a film about this whole adventure."

"You're making a movie about the stolen movies?" Nancy asked, laughing.

"Yes. Cameo Studios has already said they're interested in it," Bill said. "We'd like to film it here on the Vineyard. I hope you girls can come and visit us on location. You can be in the movie as extras."

Bess popped her head over Nancy's shoulder, her blue eyes sparkling. "Extras? In a movie?"

Nancy laughed. "I guess we can't refuse."

On the other side, Velma Ford tucked her arm through Nancy's. "That's exciting news, Bill," she said. "But just one piece of advice from an old pro: The actress you hire to play Nancy Drew should *definitely* not do her own stunts. This detective business is way too dangerous!"

THE HARDY BOYS® SERIES By Franklin W. Dixon

NANCY DREW® MYSTERY STORIES By Carolyn Keene

☐ #58: THE FLYING SAUCER MYSTERY	72320-0/$3.99	
☐ #62: THE KACHINA DOLL MYSTERY	67220-7/$3.99	
☐ #68: THE ELUSIVE HEIRESS	62478-4/$3.99	
☐ #72: THE HAUNTED CAROUSEL	66227-9/$3.99	
☐ #73: ENEMY MATCH	64283-9/$3.50	
☐ #77: THE BLUEBEARD ROOM	66857-9/$3.50	
☐ #79: THE DOUBLE HORROR OF FENLEY PLACE	64387-8/$3.99	
☐ #81: MARDI GRAS MYSTERY	64961-2/$3.99	
☐ #83: THE CASE OF THE VANISHING VEIL	63413-5/$3.99	
☐ #84: THE JOKER'S REVENGE	63414-3/$3.99	
☐ #85: THE SECRET OF SHADY GLEN	63416-X/$3.99	
☐ #87: THE CASE OF THE RISING STAR	66312-7/$3.99	
☐ #89: THE CASE OF THE DISAPPEARING DEEJAY	66314-3/$3.99	
☐ #91: THE GIRL WHO COULDN'T REMEMBER	66316-X/$3.99	
☐ #92: THE GHOST OF CRAVEN COVE	66317-8/$3.99	
☐ #93: THE CASE OF THE SAFECRACKER'S SECRET	66318-6/$3.99	
☐ #94: THE PICTURE-PERFECT MYSTERY	66319-4/$3.99	
☐ #96: THE CASE OF THE PHOTO FINISH	69281-X/$3.99	
☐ #97: THE MYSTERY AT MAGNOLIA MANSION	69282-8/$3.99	
☐ #98: THE HAUNTING OF HORSE ISAND	69284-4/$3.99	
☐ #99: THE SECRET AT SEVEN ROCKS	69285-2/$3.99	
☐ #101: THE MYSTERY OF THE MISSING MILLIONAIRES	69287-9/$3.99	
☐ #102: THE SECRET IN THE DARK	69279-8/$3.99	
☐ #104: THE MYSTERY OF THE JADE TIGER	73050-9/$3.99	
☐ #107: THE LEGEND OF MINER'S CREEK	73053-3/$3.99	
☐ #109: THE MYSTERY OF THE MASKED RIDER	73055-X/$3.99	
☐ #110: THE NUTCRACKER BALLET MYSTERY	73056-8/$3.99	
☐ #111: THE SECRET AT SOLAIRE	79297-0/$3.99	
☐ #112: CRIME IN THE QUEEN'S COURT	79298-9/3.99	
☐ #113: THE SECRET LOST AT SEA	79299-7/$3.99	
☐ #114:THE SEARCH FOR THE SILVER PERSIAN	79300-4/$3.99	
☐ #115: THE SUSPECT IN THE SMOKE	79301-2/$3.99	
☐ #116: THE CASE OF THE TWIN TEDDY BEARS	79302-0/$3.99	
☐ #117: MYSTERY ON THE MENU	79303-9/$3.99	
☐ #118: TROUBLE AT LAKE TAHOE	79304-7/$3.99	
☐ #119: THE MYSTERY OF THE MISSING MASCOT	87202-8/$3.99	
☐ #120: THE CASE OF THE FLOATING CRIME	87203-6/$3.99	
☐ #121: THE FORTUNE-TELLER'S SECRET	87204-4/$3.99	
☐ #122: THE MESSAGE IN THE HAUNTED MANSION	87205-2/$3.99	
☐ #123: THE CLUE ON THE SILVER SCREEN	87206-0/$3.99	
☐ #124: THE SECRET OF THE SCARLET HAND	87207-9/$3.99	
☐ #125: THE TEEN MODEL MYSTERY	87208-7/$3.99	
☐ #126: THE RIDDLE IN THE RARE BOOK	87209-5/$3.99	
☐ #127: THE CASE OF THE DANGEROUS SOLUTION	50500-9/$3.99	
☐ #128: THE TREASURE IN THE ROYAL TOWER	50502-5/$3.99	
☐ #129: THE BABYSITTER BURGLARIES	50507-6/$3.99	
☐ #130: THE SIGN OF THE FALCON	50508-4/$3.99	
☐ #131: THE HIDDEN INHERITANCE	50509-2/$3.99	
☐ #132: THE FOX HUNT MYSTERY	50510-6/$3.99	
☐ #133: THE MYSTERY AT THE CRYSTAL PALACE	50515-7/$3.99	
☐ #134: THE SECRET OF THE FORGOTTEN CAVE	50516-5/$3.99	
☐ #135: THE RIDDLE OF THE RUBY GAZELLE	00048-9/$3.99	
☐ #136: THE WEDDING DAY MYSTERY	00050-0/$3.99	
☐ #137: IN SEARCH OF THE BLACK ROSE	00051-9/$3.99	
☐ #138: THE LEGEND OF THE LOST GOLD	00049-7/$3.99	
☐ NANCY DREW GHOST STORIES	69132-5/$3.99	
☐ #139: THE SECRET OF CANDLELIGHT INN	00052-7/$3.99	
☐ #140: THE DOOR-TO-DOOR DECEPTION	00053-5/$3.99	
☐ #141: THE WILD CAT CRIME	00120-5/$3.99	
☐ #142: THE CASE OF CAPTIAL INTRIGUE	00751-3/$3.99	

A MINSTREL BOOK
Published by Pocket Books